Haunted

"If you like American Horror Story, you will love
Lynn Carthage's *Haunted*. Carthage delivers a spooky,
fun trip across the pond. Loved!"
—**Danielle Paige,** *New York Times* bestselling author
of *Dorothy Must Die*

"Lynn Carthage has crafted a remarkable neo-Gothic thriller
with a twist you'll never see coming."
—**Michelle Gagnon,** author of *Don't Look Now*

"Get ready for a very different type of paranormal read. Different
from your average ghost story, Carthage makes *Haunted* work by
doing a wonderful job of bringing her characters to life. Along
with the twist, there's a lovely romance, as well as a mystery . . .
Overall this is a fast, easy read that will keep you on your toes."
—*RT Book Reviews*, 4 stars

"The titular haunting is multilayered and centers on a grotesque
villain who delivers camp and true horror . . . The final
showdown . . . involves a complex chain of heroics, redemption,
and forgiveness that strikes the right chord of sincere emotion . . .
A slightly gruesome haunted house story that will appeal to
paranormal romance readers who also crave light horror."
—*School Library Journal*

"A vampiric ancestor, a selection of ghosts, an historic family
estate, an unexpected twist . . . Phoebe is a likeable heroine,
and the story moves along well. Fans of occult stories will
undoubtedly enjoy this one. This entertaining fantasy is
recommended for genre fans."
—*VOYA*

"Carthage takes a sharp, twisting turn away from the traditional haunted-house scares and happens upon something far scarier."
—*Booklist*

Betrayed

"If you're looking for a well-written, head-rolling, time-slipping ghost story, *Betrayed* is hard to beat. Carthage has a keen eye for detail, and the historical scenes are vivid and rich."
—**Madame Griselda**

"Fast-paced, with great history about Paris, clean writing, and an interesting story line that kept me guessing."
—**Gina L. Mulligan,** author of *Remember the Ladies*

"Luscious descriptions of Versailles, the ominous threat of ancient evil, and an unusual and swoon-worthy budding romance make *Betrayed* every bit as satisfying as the first book of the Arnaud Legacy."
—**Jennifer Laam,** author of *The Secret Daughter of the Tsar* and *The Tsarina's Legacy*

"Fascinatingly terrifying stuff."
—**Erin Lindsay McCabe,** author of *I Shall Be Near to You*

Avenged

The Arnaud Legacy, Book Three

LYNN CARTHAGE

KENSINGTON PUBLISHING CORP.
www.kensingtonbooks.com

KENSINGTON BOOKS are published by

Kensington Publishing Corp.
119 West 40th Street
New York, NY 10018

All Kensington titles, imprints, and distributed lines are available at special quantity discounts for bulk purchases for sales promotions, premiums, fund-raising, educational, or institutional use.

Special book excerpts or customized printings can also be created to fit specific needs. For details, write or phone the office of the Kensington sales manager: Kensington Publishing Corp., 119 West 40th Street, New York, NY 10018, attn: Sales Department; phone 1-800-221-2647.

KENSINGTON and the K logo are Reg. U.S. Pat. & TM Off.

ISBN-13: 978-1-61773-628-5
ISBN-10: 1-61773-628-7

First Trade Paperback Printing: March 2017

10 9 8 7 6 5 4 3 2 1

Printed in the United States of America

First electronic edition: March 2017

ISBN-13: 978-1-61773-631-5
ISBN-10: 1-61773-631-7

To Clara and Reid. I love you more than tongue can tell.

On a stronde the king doth slumber, and below the mede the dragon bataille the wicked brike with bisemare from yon damosel, and the goodnesse undonne for she who bitrayseth. But an thee seche they of the ilke lykenes and lygnage, for a long tyme abide thee to come thereby the thre wyghts borne on the day of swich clamor for the kynge and han them drink of Sangreçu blood, then they may leere the halkes and lede the lorn to might, eftsoone do Brytayne arise to her gloire.

—*Secret Cabals, Societies & Orders*

Avenged

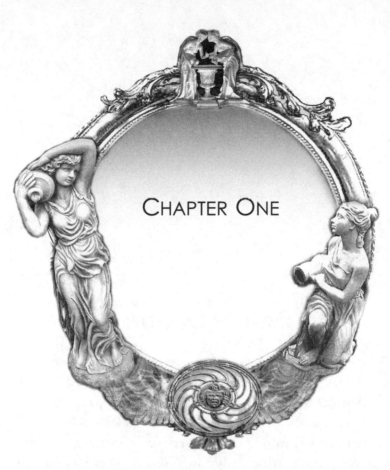

CHAPTER ONE

It is with hopes of the museum becoming a more
cosmopolitan institution that I enclose the funds herein.
Surely it will credit the facility to highlight objects of a broader
focus than the inconsequential items of a local nature. I will
assist the staff in reorganizing the collections to not appear so
provincial and brutish.

—Scrap of a letter from Reginald Q. Boswick

Told from the point of view of
ELEANOR DARROW

*T*he life of one such as me was never meant to be extraordinary. The tales my mother spun by my bedside involved princesses and ivy-twined castle walls, people whose blood beat royal in their veins even if cinders etched their faces temporarily untidy. There were never stories about servants, only about girls cruelly cast as servants until woodland creatures and love-struck princes proved it all a falsehood.

There is no glamour to a life in service. There is only waking when your bones ache and you wish you might sleep in longer, kneeling on cold, hard flagstones to clean the grease left by others, carrying heavy trays up steep, dim staircases used only by your kind. Your betters barely care what your name is. Your good work goes unnoticed; your errors earn angry shouts.

This was the world I was born into, intended for service from the moment I emerged from my mother's womb and was identified as female. The Arnaud Manor, whose influence presided over the small English town of Grenshire, was immediately my destination after I'd finished a modicum of schooling and learning my letters.

All we serving folk of Grenshire had the misfortune that the mistress of the manor, Madame Arnaud, was a woman of deep evil and committed deplorable deeds. I can scarcely account for the fact that I found hidden strength in me—the strength ordinarily assigned to princesses and not servants—and tried to kill her. I had thought my actions effective and Grenshire released, but some deeper magic, embedded in the very stones of the manor, revived her.

Thus proceeded many dark decades.

After my death, I became the subject of those begged-for tales of long ago, the wraiths who rattled their chains and tore through their death shrouds to haunt the living, the tales my mother would set princesses aside for only if her mood suited it. Rare were these sinister tales, and I became one, though my mother never knew.

Wafting down hallways was not an attractive prospect, as the manor was the place that spelled my doom, so I took to haunting a meadow where Austin and I used to tryst. Where he and I once lay on our backs looking at the clouds racing between the leaves of the trees whose cover we sought, kissing as if we had all the time in the world, now I implored the winds for deliverance.

We had never joined our bodies together, although I dreamed of marrying him. After death, the regrets that might've been hot and angry instead turned to quiet pains one bends one's body around. I wish I had given Austin everything, and he me.

By the time I met Phoebe and Miles, I had already had a century of nursing my grievances.

They showed up, skin brighter than my muted translucence. They were *fresh*; there's no other way to describe it. They still carried the vehemence of emotions that death had erased from my arsenal of feelings. They had desire for each other, and oh, my dear ages, did it hurt to see that they could have each other. In a strange way, they outwitted death. They still managed to have love.

I've come to understand that my role in our strange triad is not equal to theirs. For so long, I thought it was because I was powerless, the servant, while they came from an era in which servitude had largely subsided. But sometimes as I sit and wonder—one of the timeless activities I have eternity to perform, a verb without much sway—if perhaps my role is not equal because it is, in fact, greater.

A mind-spinning possibility.

Phoebe's family—still living, God bless them—all stand on the west lawn watching a bulldozer rip through soil that hasn't been touched since gardeners abandoned the Arnaud property eons ago.

Tabby, Phoebe's two-year-old sister, is in her mother's arms, halfway terrified but thoroughly fascinated. She periodically points at the machine (whose name, *bulldozer*, Phoebe very nicely supplied . . . I do like the idea of the mechanism being somehow related to the brute work of a bull) and then buries her face in her mother's neck.

It's very loud, but I find myself enjoying that. Death muffles so many sensations, that to hear something rip-roaring through your ears, dinning so that you want to cover them, is exhilarating. I stand smiling at the whole spectacle, the man in the broad orange hat yanking on levers, trying to make a better show for the watching family.

The earth peels away in stripes, rich loam beneath the caked surface, roots exposed and a glad smell coming up to meet our noses. In an instant, I remember my mother's cottage garden, kneeling with her to tend the weeds and smelling the soil as it came away clinging to the white roots. *Ahhhh.* I haven't thought of that in a hundred years.

"What's he doing here?" Steven, Phoebe's stepdad, yells over to his wife. I turn and stare in the direction he points.

Uh-oh.

It's Reginald Boswick.

He's one of the local Grenshire villagers. His face is red as he paces across to the bulldozer and flags its driver. He's moving very quickly; one might almost surmise he knows he will be stopped if he acts with even a degree less certainty.

"Stop your motor, sir!" he calls up to the driver.

Steven throws a look of disbelief at his wife and marches over to join Boswick. "What's the meaning of this?" he asks. "This is private property."

"I'm here on village business," says Boswick. "Cut the motor!"

The driver looks down at Steven, who nods. The man stops the engine, and the bucket of soil lurches a bit midair, getting used to the idea of not moving. In the sudden silence, I hear the single whistle of a bird.

"Steven Arnaud, I'm here to deliver an order from the Village of Grenshire, immediately halting work at this site for now or any time in the future," says Boswick. Sweaty, but bearing an expression of triumph, he brandishes an envelope, which Steven rips out of his hand.

"You've got to be kidding," mutters Steven. He rips open the envelope as the rest of us, living and dead, come to peer over his shoulder and read the paper. It bears a golden embossed seal of the village at the top and a red-stamped date. The document does indeed order the family to cease work "to, or around the environs of, the Arnaud Manor."

"Why?" asks Steven flatly.

"As I've told you before, in no uncertain terms which were nonetheless outright ignored, there is to be no digging here."

"I understand that part. The part I don't get is *why*."

I was impressed with Steven's demeanor in the face of such rudeness. He had the bearing of a gentleman of my day, a politeness that I noticed during our recent tour of the Continent seems to have evaporated from society.

"This is a powerful piece of land," says Boswick. "It ought not to be tampered with. We're protecting you from your own idiotic selves. I told you we could set you up with a very nice home in the village."

"You catch more flies with honey than with vinegar," Phoebe's mother murmurs.

"Honey doesn't work with you people!" Boswell explodes. "If I call you stupid, it's to drill home the idea, which you refuse to accept, that this property needs to be left alone."

"Excuse me," says the driver. He leans out of the elevated window of the bulldozer.

"You don't have any jurisdiction out here," says Steven. "The National Trust for Historic Preservation has reviewed all our plans and approved them."

"You're still a tax-paying property owner in Grenshire and subject to its rules."

"Its rules, yes, but not orders drawn up by off-balance citizens with their own agenda."

"I'm helping you!" roars Boswick. "This is all done to

protect you, since you're too idiotic to realize the danger you're in."

"Then *tell* us," says Phoebe's mother.

I lean in, wanting to hear the answer to her very sensible question. What exactly *is* the danger at the Arnaud estate, in his opinion?

"Excuse me," says the bulldozer driver again. "There's something you might want to see here." He opens his door and steps down from the cab, then goes to stand at the edge of the hole he's dug. He turns to look at the rest of the group expectantly.

Dully glinting in the freshly turned soil, two slender metallic objects have appeared.

The sight affects me, although I can't even tell what the objects are. My hand flies to my throat. I feel panic, rage. Emotions bolt through my bones and I hear a clamor as if from far away.

"What are those?" asks Phoebe. Her tone is too light; she doesn't feel what I do.

I shake my head and try to push away the sounds, but men still shout although I know they're not real. Or not anymore.

Miles runs both hands through his thick dark hair, as if overtaken by grief. Our eyes meet, and it is an old message we share that I don't quite understand. He steps into the hole and gestures for me to follow him.

We can't disturb the earth; our footfalls have no weight. I could've intentioned myself over to the silver objects instantly, but instead take the time to duplicate the slowed walk of the living. I'm somehow reluctant to look.

Miles and I kneel next to the silver artifacts. Now that we are so close, I can tell what they are. The din in my head resolves: I can tell that I'm hearing swords clashing in between the shouts and cries. As soon as I recognize the sounds, they fade away.

We're staring at the blades of two swords half buried, their hilts hidden.

"Odd," murmurs Phoebe. "Shouldn't swords be buried with their warriors?"

Soil has done no favors to these swords, and the edges, once lovingly sharpened by their wielders at some fireside as they told the tale of battle, have rusted and lost their crisp lines. Dirt has been attracted to the wet metal and cloyed to it. The swords are sad emblems of once-fierce men.

I look at my friends' faces. Phoebe looks intrigued in a detached way. But Miles . . . he feels the agony and bloodshed associated with these weapons. I can almost hear a howl from down the centuries, men fighting for their lives, teeth bared, their whole souls on display as blood seeps into soil.

Did I once battle in that way?

I look at my own palm, pale, soft despite my years of service, and can't imagine it clamped around a hilt.

But if I focus harder, I can almost see another hand . . . and that one is worthy of wielding a sword.

"It looks like you get your wish," says Steven, and I wake from this dream of the past. "At least for this part of the property. We'll have to stop digging and get some experts out. I'm sure archeologists are going to want to work this over."

I look at Boswick, to see if he's suitably thrilled. Instead, his face is drawn and white.

"You fool," says Boswick. He kneels in the dirt and stretches his hand toward the closest of the swords. His arm goes through my skirt.

"Don't touch that," says Phoebe's mother, Anne. "That's a historical artifact."

He ignores her. She bends down and pulls his arm back. "Maybe you didn't hear me," she says.

"Mr. Boswick, you need to leave," says Steven. "I'm going to call the proper authorities to come and look at this. In the meantime, you won. Construction has been halted."

"I can't leave now!" says Boswick.

"Oh, you will," vows Steven grimly.

In the space of months, his daughter has died and he and his family upended what remained of their lives to move to England, where he learned that his daughter was a ghost. He isn't about to suffer Boswick's stupidity. "On your feet now, or I'll get you to your car with the imprint of my shoe on the back of your pants."

Boswick complies, but takes his time to do it. He scowls up at Steven and slowly rises. "Why'd you even come here?" he mutters angrily. "You've disturbed soil that hasn't been touched in centuries."

"I came here because it's my home," says Steven. "Now get the hell out."

After Boswick leaves, Steven consults with the man who drives the bulldozer. There's a process in place to alert archeological experts whenever a construction dig encounters historical artifacts.

I approach Miles, standing directly above one of the swords.

"Do you think these swords were yours?" Phoebe asks.

It's hard to imagine, staring down at the tarnished ruins in the dirt, that I wielded one of these, particularly as a female. But I feel an undeniable pull.

"Somehow, yes," says Miles.

"And there's more here," I say, surprising myself.

"Yes," marvels Miles. "You're right."

If I focus, I can feel the untouched earth pulsing where other weapons lie.

"The archeologists are going to have a field day," says Miles.

"And Reginald Boswick is going to lose his mind," says Phoebe with a half smile.

"Don't you feel anything?" I ask Phoebe. "These swords have no effect on you?"

She shrugs. "I don't think so."

An emotion comes over me that makes me feel guilty. I'm glad she isn't linked to these swords. In the short time I've known her and Miles, they have displayed powers that I'm not given, traveled through the centuries in a voyage that wasn't offered to me, and far worse . . . I despise myself for thinking this, for the low pettiness within me . . . they are connected by love, and I have been the outsider in this trio. For once, it is nice to be the person who is included while someone else is excluded.

"I wish I could move the soil myself," says Miles. "Here, and here, and . . ." He continues pointing around the overgrown plot. "It will take the archeologists forever to see the pattern."

"There's a pattern?" asks Phoebe.

Oh yes, it seems the bits of iron lie in a ceremonial circle, roughly drawn across the yard.

"A circle," Miles answers her.

"It's interesting you would've had a sword, Eleanor," says Phoebe to me. "You must've been a woman warrior."

I'm tempted to correct her, but I don't know the truth

myself, just a gut-level rejection of her words. I don't bother to say anything, because there isn't anything to say.

"Pretty impressive," says Miles with a wink at me. That wink undoes me every time. I wish he wouldn't do it. He belongs to Phoebe, and that shared, secretive flirting gives me a lurch of false hope.

"What do you think they'll do with the objects after they process them?" asks Phoebe.

"They'll probably go to the museum in Rookmoor," says Miles.

"There's a museum?" I ask. Miles looks disconcerted.

"Yes. I suppose it was established after you died. I went when I was nine years old, as part of a school trip."

Phoebe grins at me and shakes her head slightly as she looks over at Miles. "Given that the past is trying to tell us things, don't you think it would be a good idea for us to visit?"

Miles looks embarrassed. "Of course, I should've thought of that long ago. It just didn't strike me as important. It's a lot of broken pots and old stuff."

"I'm going to kill you if the answer to all our questions is on display in a big glass case," says Phoebe.

He straightens up and gives her that magisterial look I adore. Strong Miles. "It would've been your fault for not enquiring. Plus, as it pains me to add, it's impossible to kill someone who's already dead."

"My fault for not enquiring?" sputters Phoebe.

"You *are* the Arnaud in our trio," I say, bolstering Miles's playful jab. "It falls upon you to lead us in asking the pertinent questions."

"Listen, if I'm the leader, this whole mission is doomed," says Phoebe. "But maybe our local tour guide here could show us the museum. You know, if you felt like it, Miles, and if the timing was right for us to learn stuff. Or we could just hang around and haunt the mansion for a few hundred years, like Eleanor."

I step back. Her joke went too far. She's only been dead awhile and can't imagine what it was like all these years, helplessly stuck in a region of no rest. Miles opens his mouth and I can tell he's about to stick up for me, but before he can say anything, I feel Phoebe's arms around me, tight.

"I'm sorry," she whispers. "I didn't think before I said that."

I hug her back, amazed how nice it feels and how strangely right after my lifetime of not even thinking of touching my superiors in such an informal way, I perform a quick mental correction. She's not my superior. We're equals.

"It's fine, miss," I hear myself say before I can bite back the automatic *miss*.

"Thank you, miss," she says back, and I smile at her gentle rebuff of my maid's language.

"Well, let's hit the museum and solve all the world's evil problems," says Miles.

"At least those in England," says Phoebe.

"Or maybe just those in Grenshire," I say. "Let's be realistic."

We use intention to move to the museum. I've never been to Rookmoor. In my lifetime, the ten miles between it and Grenshire might as well have included an ocean. We're on the front steps of a white stone building with columns. As I turn to look behind us, I see many cars chortling along and people walking quickly, chatting aggressively on their mobiles. I feel as nervous as I did in Paris, learning about crowds for the first time. When I was alive, the largest grouping of people I'd ever seen was the line of servants when we queued up for inspections, the head housekeeper checking our hair for lice and appropriately starched caps, ensuring our uniforms and aprons were fastidiously clean.

"Let's go in," says Phoebe, and again we intention, through the heavy glass doors into the lobby.

I love these spaces so much, the places where people have chosen to preserve certain things of the past. Sometimes they are the most valuable things, gold laden and set with jewels, but just as often they are the things used in daily life that gain significance by no longer being used. In Paris, I trailed after Phoebe's family into several museums and found it fascinating to be confronted by objects I knew well, that had to be explained by a note card by the exhibit.

Here in Rookmoor, few people are visiting—immediate relief for me. We walk from glass case to glass case. We see many objects from the Iron Age history of this area, things farmers dug up while plowing fields: clasps to hold a cloak snug around someone's neck, bits of nails that once held something together.

Miles races ahead of me and Phoebe. He doesn't linger to read the plaques; he's far more interested in finding something that makes our work pay off. Whatever that may look like. It's probably not pieces of broken pottery and delicate plates from a porcelain factory that once thrived here, but I'm still curious enough to pause and learn more, as is Phoebe.

Miles returns as I'm admiring a pearl choker that one of our wealthier citizens wore to the local Queen Victoria's Jubilee celebration, sadly unattended by the monarch herself.

"There's nothing here about the Arnaud Manor," he says.

"There was probably a great diorama, and Reginald Boswick had it taken down," jokes Phoebe.

"It's so strange there's nothing here to note its presence," I say. "The Arnaud Manor was the center of our lives. If one didn't work there, one at least lived off the wages of a family member that did."

"Everyone's trying to pretend it never existed," says Miles. "They let it grow over with weeds, and blocked the driveway, and hoped the truth would die when the oldest generation does."

"Except that there are still rumors about it," says Phoebe. "You told me about Madame Arnaud when you found out I'd just moved here."

"Yeah, kids talked about it at school, especially around Halloween," says Miles.

"It's a difficult task to completely suppress the fact of an enormous manor and its hundreds of occupants and servants," I say.

"And yet the museum is trying," says Miles.

I nod sadly. It's too bad. We need help, unless the universe plans for us to stay ghosts forever . . . and I can't imagine that it does. We have some kind of task to perform, and I have to fervently believe that once we do it, we'll be released to rest in peace, just like the tombstones promise.

"Well, let's keep looking anyway," says Phoebe. "Even if there isn't anything labeled 'Arnaud,' there might be something that can help us. Eleanor, you especially should look at everything since you were part of the household when it was still in operation."

They both look at me, smiling, and I feel gratified by their trust. "All right," I say. "I'll continue looking."

There are several alcoves off the main exhibit hall, and I look thoroughly through all the ones on the west side.

"Nothing?" asks Phoebe. She's stayed at my elbow the whole time although Miles has left to do another brisk round.

"I'm afraid not," I say.

Yet, in the second alcove on the east side, I see something I recognize.

It's a wooden chair from the Arnaud Manor, a small and unassuming one, lightweight with a ladder back and an embroidered cushion seat. The embroidery shows wildflowers arranged in a large wreath. I approach the chair with my eyes growing moist.

"Are you okay?" asks Phoebe.

I don't trust myself to speak. This chair holds so many memories. It was stationed in a quiet hallway, a relatively private place once everyone was hard at work. Austin and I would sit there and steal a few kisses when we could. Austin worked in the Arnaud stables and had rarely set foot in the house until we met—then he used any manner of excuse to find his way in.

The chair did something special besides providing a place for us to linger. When weight was placed on the cushion—whenever someone sat on it, that is—a click sounded from the chair's interior and a brief, whirring sound came as some sort of mechanism prepared itself. And then: music.

The chair was a sort of music box. It played a short, charming air. The first time Austin sat on it and it began playing, he'd shrieked and leapt up, the music ceasing the instant he rose. It was lovely, later, to kiss with that chiming accompaniment.

As I stare at the chair now, I want fiercely to hear the song again, to be on Austin's lap, winding my arms around his neck. It's so desolate to see it with a golden rope stretched across it with a large placard reading DO NOT TOUCH. That chair deserves to be sat on, to have laughter ring out at the surprise of its voice . . . and now it sits in a dim corner, unused and unappreciated.

The placard for the chair says, "Folk art seat cushion from Grenshire, an example of the cunning needlework once displayed by capable seamstresses. The mechanical chair plays the air 'My Lady Cries for Her Love' when the cushion is depressed."

So that's what the song was called.

"You have seen this chair before?" Phoebe asks.

I nod. My heart is aching now, for a lad with a quick smile and drowsy eyes, a way with horses and a way with me.

"Was this Madame Arnaud's chair?" asks Miles. He has apparently noticed my and Phoebe's staring at it.

"No," I say. "She would never sit in something so plain. This was something pretty for the servants. I have no idea where it came from, and I don't think it's important. It's just that . . ."

"What?"

"I used to . . ." I choke out a sob.

I feel Phoebe's arm go around my shoulder as she presses me into her side.

"Leave her alone," she says.

It's nice to be released from the duty of explaining. I try to get hold of my emotions. I turn away as I rub my eyes, and I see several other objects from the Arnaud household.

A standing lamp with an intricate stained glass lampshade. A statue of a nymph in love with her own outthrust hip. A wardrobe of white and gold that looks like it could've been from Versailles, although of course Madame Arnaud would've never taken such a large object with her when she fled to England.

I stoop and read each of the cards through my tears, blinking them back as best I can. Not a single one says anything about where these objects came from, other than "Grenshire." The name *Arnaud* is not mentioned.

I stand up straight and look at Miles and Phoebe, regarding me with sad faces.

"I'll be fine," I say. "That chair just walloped me in a spot still tender. Austin and I used to sit there. These other objects are from the Arnaud household as well, although not one of them mentions that fact on the descriptions."

"Why are they here?" asks Phoebe. "I remember that one wing of the house was completely empty, but the other wing was still filled with her furnishings."

I try to cast my mind back.

"When the servants left." I falter. "They may have . . . taken things and destroyed things. They were furious."

"You, too?" asks Miles.

"I wasn't there," I say.

I look one last time at the chair. "My Lady Cries for Her Love"—how apt that that was its tune.

CHAPTER TWO

The terror of being buried alive led, for some, to the quaint
custom of installing bells above tombs, to be rung via a string
leading directly into the coffin. What terror for the night
watchman to hear the tolling across the fog-swept cemetery!

—*Victorian Funerary Customs*

*T*he walls of the church are large river stones snugly fitted together. Arched windows hold stained glass with scenes so dusty they are difficult to discern now. To the side is the churchyard, with newer tombstones at the front, the etched names still sharp, the flowers in the metal vases fresh. They will run out of plots in another fifty years, I think.

At the back, where the grass gets more tufty and the stones tilt from settling in the ground, the older residents of the cemetery lie. I pick my way through, seeing surnames I remember, giving me a jolt. I hadn't thought about these people for centuries. With some names, a face floats up in memory, distinct, even words they have said to me coming from their lips, and for others only the name remains as the basis of my recollection.

"Do you know exactly where he is?" Miles asks. I imagine he, too, is seeing names he knows, from long-dead relatives and friends of his grandparents.

"Back here somewhere," I say vaguely. I had followed Austin for a while after I died, but it proved painful. I'm aware I will no doubt see *Husband of . . .* etched on his stone and learn the name of some woman who took my place. I feel like I have visited his gravesite before, but I'm not certain. It wasn't a place of vigil for me. By the time Austin died, I would've long given up on the idea we could somehow be reunited. If I did visit, it would've been in a scourge of tears, and I might not have truly seen it.

"Can you use intention to get there?" Phoebe asks. It would make sense; all I have to do is picture the stone. I sigh and give an attempt. Valiantly, I try to see the grave I am not even sure I've visited.

But instantly, I feel my stomach swoop down, the sensation that accompanies intention.

"Well done, Eleanor!" says Miles, but it is Phoebe who has sense enough to give me a pitying look.

Here we are.

The tomb of my lover, whom I never got to love fully.

It's a plain gray stone, on the small side, but there does appear to be an incredible amount of writing and embossing on it. Moss has covered the indents of the letters and symbols. Of all of us, only Phoebe might be able to pull it away from the stone, but she gamely tries without success. So I kneel before it and try to "translate" through the veil of clinging greenery.

His full name.

I hadn't thought about his surname in so many years. It might've become mine had the world gone my way.

He, Austin Fairecloth, and me his wife, Eleanor Fairecloth.

His birth and death dates. These numbers are hard to see, so small, and sixes look like eights look like nines. I give up on that.

With patience, I try to figure out the words that mark his passing. *Dear son and hopeful heir to the promises of the old . . .*

"Does that last word say *reign?*" Phoebe asks hopefully.

"I think so."

I'm mystified. "If he was important in the same way that we're important," I say slowly, "why did he die?"

"You're one hundred percent sure he died permanently?" Miles asks.

I look at him earnestly. "If there were the slightest chance that Austin still roamed this world in the merest shadow of a manner, I would know it."

"I'm so used to thinking of us as an enchanted trio. How do we add a fourth?" Phoebe says.

I nod. There are so many ancient precedents for a rule of three.

"Maybe he would've only been heir by being allied with you," Miles suggests.

"Magical marriage," I say. "The sealing together of our separate powers."

"Did he seem like he had powers when he was alive?" Phoebe asks.

I pause. "Not that I recall. His family, though, as I've told you . . . they were deeply knowledgeable about the old wisdom here, the pagan past of Grenshire."

"Maybe they *wanted* him to be powerful, their only son, so they invented their own mythology over his being an heir somehow?" she asks.

"Maybe."

"And that would mean the 'clues' on this tombstones are just the grandiose wishes of forlorn parents," says Miles.

"We're making a big assumption here, that his parents created the language of the tombstone. Most children outlive their parents," Phoebe points out.

Which leads us to look for the nearby stones for his parents. It is only a few paces away. One stone for the both of them: Charles and Elsabeth Fairecloth. Unlike Austin's tomb, it is a straightforward one that only remarks birth and death dates, and the legend *Rest in Peace*. I study the death dates, easier because this stone, removed from the shade of the willow, gets more sunlight and isn't as covered by moss.

Charles died five years before his wife, so there wasn't a catastrophic event that took them both. I stride back to Austin's stone to better scry his death year.

"If only I could just dig my fingernail in and remove this one bit of moss," I say.

I close my eyes in frustration. There was a period of time, all too brief, when Phoebe and Miles could've come here and scraped the moss away, giving us all sorts of information. Yet they squandered it. They drank of the Sangreçu vials, whether sacred or unholy, and explored each other's bodies like lust-driven peasants in a hayloft. The *good* that they could've done while their bodies worked! We might be so much closer to understanding our mission, so much closer to the peace that these tombstones promise.

"It doesn't matter," says Phoebe. "Don't worry—it's still helpful anyway. We know at least *someone* thought that Austin was—"

"It does matter," I say, interrupting her. "Austin may be the key to everything, and we can't even read the bloody words on his tombstone!"

I blush, luckily with my face unseen by all but the inscrutable words on the stone, deeply ashamed of my foul language.

I also want to recall the foolhardy nature of my words.

Austin isn't the key to anything except my own broken heart. He's not here centuries later like I am. He was a regular man who died and decayed like the world expects us to.

"I'm sorry," whispers Phoebe.

I stand up, head whirling, ready to retreat. I want to leave Phoebe and Miles to themselves, to their love they got to have, lucky fools, and return to the meadow where I've spent much of the time since my death. I love the calm of a wind lightly moving the grasses, the tree gaining height each season.

"I'm going to go," I say quietly. "This is all just a bit much for me, isn't it. I'll just . . ."

Miles gently puts his hands on my shoulders. "There's one other way to look," he says.

"What do you mean?"

"We could look at Austin. Or you could."

He's wincing as he says it, and Phoebe reaches from the side to push his hands off me. "No!" she says fiercely. "How could you ever suggest such a thing?"

"What is he suggesting?" I ask.

As of one accord, they both look down. It's not just shame: they're looking between their feet at the plot where Austin lies.

Oh dear.

They mean for me to intention down and look at Austin in his coffin.

"I can't," I whisper.

"I know you can't," says Phoebe comfortingly.

But they're right. What if Austin was buried with a clue? We should look. Leave no gravestone unturned.

"I can do it for you," says Miles.

With relief, I'm about to accept, but it seems wrong. Austin is *mine*. It would be like asking a stranger to wash his body after death. I shake my head to release that thought: it must've been Austin's wife who performed that duty. Although . . .

"He didn't marry, did he?" I ask wildly. "There's no stone for a wife?" I trot to look at all the nearby tombs. "They would've marked it on his gravestone, and they didn't! There's no word of anyone else!"

I sink to my knees in exult. Austin kept himself apart, in my memory! He chose no other!

Phoebe joins me on her knees as well. It strikes me that we hold the posture of mourning, and exult quickly turns to sadness, the enduring emotion of all my centuries.

"It's my job to do," I say.

"If you're sure," says Phoebe.

We both rise. "We'll be right here," says Miles.

"Of course we'll be right here. What a stupid thing to say!" snaps Phoebe. "As if we're going to wander off and leave her."

"I love your loyalty," I say to her, and the words attain a certain darkness in the air between us. There was a time she was not loyal to me. She betrayed me in such a profound way, maybe when we borrowed other bodies, when we were other living creatures with different names. Her betrayal, I privately believe, is one of the reasons we yet walk this earth without substance. We need to unwind her treachery.

I walk back to Austin's grave. I know it will change much, to see the stark bones he has disintegrated into. I remember him lively, sweet, funny, with ruddy cheeks and a warm, fast mouth that made kindling out of me. Large hands, a gentle voice for the horses, but a good, low, strong one for me and . . . oh my Lord, the things he used to say to me, while the chair plinked out its plaintive air . . .

"We can come back later when you're more prepared," says Phoebe. "Nothing says we have to do it today."

I smile at her. "Centuries have passed, my dear Phoebe," I say. "I need to be stout of heart."

I cross my hands before me, as if penitent, and bow my head. I think of Austin's coffin and intention myself there.

There's no light down here and I can't see a thing.

I'm aware of an old smell—not disgusting, but unpleasant. Austin's bones have long ago shed tissue, muscle, skin. He is dry and long abandoned by the worms as a meal well picked over.

I reach out to where his body should be within the confines of his wooden coffin, but again touch eludes me. My heart feels heavy. I hadn't expected fireworks down here, but it's a dismal truth that Austin truly is dust, and we will likely never reunite.

"I miss you," I whisper to the man I can't see. "You should've married someone else. It wouldn't have been a betrayal. And yet . . . I'm so glad you didn't."

No response in this claustrophobic, dark space.

"Well, good-bye, then," I say. I linger just in case he was rallying forces, rousing himself after all this slumber, but he remains silent.

I don't shed any tears. He's been dead so long he's really just a lovely illustration in a book I've kept on a shelf, unread despite its once being a favorite.

I rise back up to join Miles and Phoebe.

"Anything?" asks Miles.

"Nothing," I say, not without some bitterness. "It's pitch-black down there, and I don't have the power of touch."

"We noticed something," says Phoebe. She beckons me around to the back of Austin's stone. Just above the line of wild grass, a round engraving has been cut into his tombstone. It's the dragon emblem we've seen before, including carved into Austin's own door.

"My God," I breathe.

The symbol shows a dragon trapped in a cell, his wings pressing against the ceiling and both sides. His mouth is open in an enraged roar, and between his splayed claws is a sword he's dropped.

A sword.

"One of the swords at the manor," I blurt, "could well be the dragon's!"

"Yes!" says Phoebe. "There has to be a connection."

"Please," says Miles. "You don't seriously believe in dragons?"

"Maybe a dragon as metaphor," I say. "A valiant warrior so fierce he seems to breathe fire."

"And that was Austin?" Phoebe asks. "He's trapped here in the grave like the dragon's trapped in the cell?"

I shake my head. "Austin was nothing like a warrior. He could calm a horse just by a few words to it. He never fought, not even with his fists, let alone a sword."

"So maybe someone Austin once was, the same way we seem to be enacting older lives," says Miles.

"Maybe," I say, but even I hear the dubiousness in my voice. I'd *love* it if Austin was part of this and I'd see him again . . . but his story seems to be long over.

CHAPTER THREE

A knight's arming sword would be passed down from father
to son, on through many generations, with repairs and
ornamentation added to keep the sword distinctive and sharp.

—www.swordlore.com

*P*hoebe insists that we check in on Tabby, so we do. She's stacking alphabet blocks on the kitchen floor as her mother cooks. The stack is nearly as high as Tabby. I study the letters as they ascend, to see if she's accidentally spelled something. No such luck.

"You took a shower at this hour?" Phoebe's mum says to Steven as he comes into the kitchen, touching his wet hair.

I reel at the difference between the cemetery we've just vacated and the doughy freshness of Tabby's skin. She's un-molded, unshaped. Even her sister's death hasn't changed her basic brightness. Her mum lifts her up to place another block, as she can no longer reach.

I wince at the clatter of blocks hitting the linoleum, and without even thinking about it intention back to the graveyard. It turns out I'm not the only one with this self-preservative instinct.

Miles, Phoebe, and I stand silently looking at the time-blasted stones of the church in the distance, listening to a cold wind rattling what's left of the dried leaves still clinging to branches and peremptorily shuffling the ones on the ground to a new place.

"So the elephant in the room . . ." says Phoebe. "You two must be buried here, right?"

"I guess so," says Miles. "I've been trying not to think about it."

"Maybe you have a symbol on your stone, too," she says.

Unspoken among all of us is an idea that sprawls until it is a vast ocean of black, turbulent water. If I sank down to look at Austin's bones, should *Miles* sink down to look at his? And would I do the same? It doesn't bear thinking about.

"The archeologist excavates his own bones," says Miles in a hollow voice.

"It'll take just a moment," I say to Miles. "We should do it. And maybe Phoebe should even intention back to the United States to look at hers. You can't see anything; it's black down there."

Miles looks relieved. "If we can't see anything, what's the point of checking? Until we have access to a light source . . . that we can, you know, *hold* . . ."

I pause to consider. Phoebe can touch Arnaud family items, original old things in the manor, but I don't think there is a portable light source she could bring into the grave with her. She could bring a candle but has no way to light it.

"So that makes it easier," I say. "A quick down-and-back to make sure there isn't something that grabs at us."

"Poor choice of words, don't you think?" he asks.

"My mom says I forget to dot my i's and cross my t's," says Phoebe. "Just in case our graves offer information, we should check. Should we all intention and report back here in thirty seconds?"

Miles turns his back on us and seems to be scanning the churchyard. "The problem for me," he says, "is I'm not sure where my stone is. Intention only works when we can picture where we're going or who we're going to."

Phoebe sighs. "We sure spend a lot of time combing through cemeteries."

She's right. Cemeteries have been a big part of our lives now. Behind the Arnaud Manor is a large plot where generations of Arnauds lie, guarded over by epic statues of grief-stricken angels. Then behind *that* is the horror of the Arnaud family, a second hidden cemetery for the child victims of Madame Arnaud. I wonder if Reginald Boswick's protests about renovations at the manor are really about that secret being discovered. Other teens our age are glued to their mobile screens, and we seem to be glued to collections of dead people arranged in rows.

We walk back to the area where newer graves have been dug. I try to keep a positive demeanor as we look for Miles's final resting place, a strategy that served me well as I performed so many thankless tasks during my life as a maid. Scraping cinders out of a cold fireplace each day, carrying heavy trays up narrow stairs while trying not to trip on my own skirts, wielding a broom until my palms adopted the shape of the handle . . . and throughout all of it I tried to sing a song inside my head to keep myself cheerful through all the drudgery. Often, the song was "The Lady Cries for Her Love." Because there is no angry mistress now to object, I hum the song openly, something that previously I could do only in the kitchens and back passageways of the manor where the mistress couldn't hear.

"That's a pretty song," says Phoebe, looking over at me.

I smile back. "It's the song the chair played. My song with Austin."

"It's a . . . haunting tune," says Miles, and Phoebe thrusts her hip sideways at his, hard enough to knock him off course until he catches his balance back.

"Sorry, Eleanor!" he says with a grin.

"Cheeky lot, you!" I say.

This is one thing Miles and Phoebe have taught me: how to rise up out of anger or despair by playfulness. I don't tell them much about my life, but I was never as light of heart as they are, easily, without effort. The way she can jokingly shove him is so profoundly far from how I would've been able to treat Austin . . . I remember the first time we touched, I thought I was going to break into a million glass pieces. Which is not to say that Austin and I were always deadly serious with each other. Far from it. We both felt giddy with the risk we took, kissing in the chair and open to being discovered. We each would've lost our place instantly had we been found by the wrong people. Yet the ease with which Miles and Phoebe swing their arms around each other's shoulders is foreign to me. Maybe it's their generation and not just their personalities. I wouldn't know. I haven't had access to normal, living people for . . . I don't want to do this math again. It's too sad.

Miles's grave proves easy to find. It's one of the few festooned with fresh flowers. Grenshire isn't a large village, so a death and burial is, I presume, a big event. It seems the entire town has left flowers for him, riotous colors, blooms that clash with each other colorwise.

"Oh shite," he says.

"Just do it quickly," Phoebe urges. "We'll wait here for you. Go!"

He groans and is gone.

I look at Phoebe, but she won't meet my glance. I take her hand, though, and she squeezes it.

In another second, he's back.

"You all right?" she asks.

He walks rapidly away from us, his hand rubbing at his face.

"Oh no," says Phoebe.

Many paces away, he pauses and waits for us to catch up. "You're not going to do that," he says grimly to Phoebe. "I died too recently," he says. "It's awful in there. And there's nothing to see anyway, like Eleanor says."

I clap my hand to my mouth. Poor Miles. He's decomposing still, and it must've smelled horrific. Austin's body was long ago decayed to nothing but dry bones.

"I get it," says Phoebe. "I'm sorry."

"Kind of gets you off the hook, doesn't it?" he laughs, but a little too loudly, too forced.

"But you . . ." he says, pointing to me with one eyebrow raised.

"Where are you, Eleanor?" asks Phoebe.

Such an odd question. *I'm* here, but my body is somewhere else.

"I don't know," I say. "I had thought I'd be near Austin, maybe, but there was no true connection between us as we never wed."

"Well, then, surely you're buried near your parents and the rest of your family," says Miles.

"All right, yes," I say. I vaguely recall placing flowers on my grandmother's grave while my mother wept openly, kneeling before the stone. "Over here, perhaps?" I start heading back toward the older part of the cemetery, where Austin is.

But an hour later, we've walked every path in this churchyard, stared at stones under which my parents and siblings lie, scoured the words on every hard-to-read stone, and have concluded I'm just not here.

"I'm somewhere else," I say simply.

"Okay," says Phoebe.

"I just don't know . . . where."

We return to look at the swords in the ground. What else can we do? I've tried to find where my family put me, but my mind isn't cooperating.

Once again I feel a pull from the ancient metal pulsing under the ground. Curious, I look at Miles.

"Are you drawn to a particular one?" I ask.

"These are other people's swords," he says decisively.

"Wouldn't each warrior's family have kept the sword? Why are they all here?" asks Phoebe.

Suddenly, someone's at my shoulder. "Oh my God!" he yells into my ear. I bolt backward, startled. "You can hear me!" he shouts.

"Of course she can hear you; you're screaming in her face!" says Miles. "Back off!"

"But you can hear me! No one has been able to hear me!" He jumps in front of Phoebe, waving his arms wildly.

"I see you," she says drily, yet she looks at me with a bit of compassion. This young man is a ghost who hasn't realized yet that he's a ghost.

He's dressed much like Miles or the people we saw in France, wearing the casual blue trousers I've learned are called jeans, a black shirt, and a baseball hat placed backward on his head. What I glean from his appearance is that he died very recently. He's not an old worn-out ghost; he's new. And with newness comes panic.

"No one's been able to see me!" he says in a tone of complete disbelief and anger. His eyes roll around as if the heavens could offer him an explanation. "This is the most crazy shite—you noticed it?"

"It's crazy, all right," comments Phoebe. "What's your name?"

"You're American!" he says. And then to me, "Why are you dressed like that?"

I'm the last holdout of the Arnaud Manor servant ghosts, hundreds of us at one time, but they were released from their otherworldly duties a few months ago. As of now, I'm the only one in a long black gown covered by a white apron. "Halloween's over! But where's the party? I'm totally in!" He takes a few steps to get closer to me, a big smile lighting up his face. At this closer range, I can see strange cuts all over his face marked by a thin line of blood. He looks like he's been ritually cut. Curious, I step closer to see the markings better, and his hands clamp down on my shoulders.

"Let go of her," says Phoebe.

"I'm Alexander," he tells me, his voice lowered as if we're alone in some quiet hallway of the manor rather than out on the grounds with Miles and Phoebe hovering close by. "What's your name?"

"Miss Eleanor Darrow, sir," I say, popping off an automatic curtsy. As soon as I do it, hot shame rushes through me and I shake off his hands on my shoulders, stepping back and running hands over my hair, tucked tidily into a long braid that runs all the way down my back.

He laughs uproariously as if this were part of an act, and probably it does seem so. "You doing a show here?" he asks.

He thinks I'm an actress filming something at the manor.

"Yes," Miles jumps into the conversation. "A BBC program called *Clueless at the Manor.* You've watched it, I'm sure?"

"I think so," Alexander nods. "I think my flatmates watch it. It's good. You're my favorite character." He leers at me.

"Stuff off," I want to tell him. I've had some experience with young men, old, too, showing an interest and thinking that a maid won't fight back, that liberties can be taken. But the only kisses from me have always been given, not taken, and the recipient was always Austin.

"Yes, she gets star billing," says Miles smoothly, with a wink at Phoebe. "And her trailer is twice the size of ours. Did you see the excavation here, with the swords being unearthed?"

"The whole town's talking about it!" he hoots. "That's why I came out. Had to slip past a whole bunch of security, so I came through the woods."

It's funny—as soon as he says the word *woods*, his whole demeanor changes. His eyes go wild and his body shakes.

"Are you quite all right?" I ask.

"Did you guys see all that?" he asks.

"See what?"

"That shite in the woods!"

"Nooo," I say slowly. "What did you see?"

"Don't go in there," he says urgently. His head swivels around as if he's afraid he's being pursued.

"You were hurt in the woods," says Phoebe gently.

He laughs but his face is in a snarl. "Hurt," he says. "Funny way to put it, isn't it?"

"We understand," says Phoebe. "We're the same way."

"It got you, too?"

"We were 'got' in different ways," says Phoebe. I see her take a deep breath. "I drowned, Miles was in an accident, and we're not totally sure what happened to Miss Darrow over here." She winks at me, but it doesn't have the same impact as when Miles does it, which feels like some vaporous hand has reached into my stomach and given it a good squeeze.

"You drowned?" he repeats. "But they pulled you out and gave you mouth-to-mouth resuscitation?"

"No," says Phoebe. "They didn't pull me out in time."

"But you . . . you're here," he says.

"Yes," she says simply.

His hands clamp on either side of his head. "No, no, no," he says. "It's too much. I need to get home." He looks briefly down at the swords in the pit. "They're cool and all, but so not worth it. Crap, I shouldn't have come!" He walks off a few paces, but returns. "Why don't you guys go with me?"

He's scared to go by himself. He was attacked somehow, but what on earth happened? We've squashed the evil at the manor, so what's still around to kill anyone?

The powers unleashed by the swords, I think to myself quietly. Maybe Reginald Boswick really did have his heart in the right place.

"We need to stay here at the manor," says Miles. "But we want to know what happened to you."

Alexander lets out a peal of hysterical laughter. "I'm fine!" he says. "I'm totally fine. I just need a beer. Or ten. I'm going to go home and raid the refrigerator. You should come. I want to get out of here. I've got to go, man!"

"Where were you when everything happened?" asks Phoebe.

"Weird shite goes down in those woods, let me tell you!" says Alexander. "But I'm okay. I've got to get going, though."

"Can you show us where?" Phoebe asks.

"No way," he says, shivering. "I want to go home."

Since Alexander seems drawn to me, I know I need to try to talk to him. "I know you saw something scary," I say. "Can you tell us what it was?"

Tears of terror spring into his eyes. "You keep asking!" he says. "Please, just let me go home."

I look at Phoebe. What next? I can't be cruel enough to keep him here against his will.

"Alexander," she says. "There's a way you can be home instantly. You don't have to walk through the woods, you don't have to walk at all. We call it *moving by intention.* All you have to do is picture the place you want to be. But I should warn you that home isn't going to—"

He's gone.

She sighs.

"Well, looks like he's an instant champ at intention," says Miles.

"What do you think happened to him?" I ask. "Did you see the cuts on his face?"

Phoebe shudders. We all pause, sifting through the chaotic and brief encounter with Alexander. One thing, though, is clear. He was hurt and died here on the Arnaud property, and we need to let Phoebe's parents know . . . because we have to protect Tabby.

We intention to the apartment of Phoebe's family, sitting modern and clean in the middle of the otherwise-destroyed-by-time manor. I wonder if, after renovations are complete, the family intends to actually live in the grand, older part. Madame Arnaud had no trouble presiding over the hundreds of rooms, but I don't know if Phoebe's family will feel comfortable doing so.

They're sitting down to dinner. I guess we spent a lot more time wandering through the churchyard than I thought. It's hard to get a sense of time of day in the modern apartment because many of the rooms have no windows, set inside the larger manor house almost like nesting boxes.

Tabby sits in a high chair, and her stout fingers fish out elements of the meal as she disregards the plastic spoon on the tray.

"Mom would've never let me do that," says Phoebe. "Tabby's too old to be eating with her fingers."

I don't say a word. There are many things Tabby's going to get away with in life, from her parents' pure relief that she's still alive.

"That's messy, Tabby," says Phoebe. She settles in next to her sister, crouching over to whisper in her ear, "Use your spoon."

Tabby keeps blithely eating. She doesn't notice Phoebe. This is the way it works—penetrating to her has usually required time and persistence.

"Tabby, we need to tell Mom and Steven something," says Phoebe. "Can you help me get them a message?"

"What will that message be?" Miles asks. "Maybe we should work it out first. We don't need to tell a toddler that some dead kid's wandering around with cuts all over his face."

"I'm just going to tell them to stay out of the woods," says Phoebe. "That's good enough, don't you think?"

She appeals to me. "It's a good start," I say. "We don't want to alarm them. Perhaps also tell them to stay away from the unearthed swords, since they seem to be connected somehow."

"Woods and swords: no good," says Phoebe. "Got it."

Tabby is now drinking out of her sippy cup, a marvelous invention if ever I did see one, and Phoebe recommences calling into her ear. "Tabby! Tabby! I need to talk to you."

These moments have come to vex me. Tabby loves her sister dearly, and is the sole member of her family who can sense her, but she isn't always attentive to the idea that her sister is around. She's caught up in her childish thoughts and fancies. Who ever knows what's in the mind of a child, but she seems always caught up in things that don't matter: begging for tiny crackers in animal shapes, loudly asking to be put down.

There was a brief period of time when Miles and Phoebe were visible to everyone. They drank from hidden vials and became Sangreçu. Until the effects wore off, they were able to talk with their families and explain the horrible, unknown task we are meant to perform without fully comprehending what that task might actually be.

They drank without me. I wasn't there, and they didn't save me any.

I try not to think about it because they are my only friends after all these many years of haunting the manor and speaking fruitfully with no one. Most of the servant ghosts were stuck, more than Tabby, in their own small wants and self-recriminations, while I couldn't bear to talk to the child ghosts. I'm grateful Miles and Phoebe are here now. It's been like a feast set before me after years of eating crumbs.

Yet . . . when my mind wanders there, I could be fit to sob for their lack of bringing me into the fold. I could've been Sangreçu, too.

Who would I have talked to anyway? Anyone I knew or

loved is long dead. But it is more the betrayal that stings than the actual loss of being temporarily able to cross over the thin veil between the living and the dead.

There's more, too.

Although Miles and Phoebe can no longer communicate with the living, the Sangreçu blood still runs in their veins and makes them special.

"Tabby?" Phoebe urges. "Can't you hear me? I'm here!"

My emotions master me, and I decide to leave. I throw Miles a glance, and he nods. He can tell. He knows I'm sad.

I intention to the front courtyard of the manor, the cobblestones now touched with pools of blackness, shadows that have fallen while we were inside. I walk to the side lawn, where orange cones encircle the area where the swords were found. A sign has been posted by an archeological authority, warning people to stay out. The bulldozer sits abandoned, its scoop sadly lying on the grass like a dog rests his head on the ground.

I'm troubled by the fact that I have no idea where I'm buried.

I must've known sometime.

I must've . . .

I decide that I want to return to the place that has held the most happiness for me in the years since I died, a meadow between the Arnaud Manor and Austin's family's cottage.

It's wind blasted; any flower that thrives here is hardy and saucy, heads dipping insolently in a breeze that would unpetal others. I love this space. It is a meadow set apart, with a privacy naturally arranged by the growth of bush and tree and wild hedge. I can't remember when I first started coming here . . . I'm not even really sure why it's special to me.

I sink down into a perturbed rest. I can never sleep. That

is a privilege for the living. But I try to rest my thoughts, let my mind fall blank.

A memory inserts itself.

I have endlessly replayed the events of my life in my mind to the degree that they fail to arouse my interest, even after pain has faded. But this memory . . .

It's about the meadow.

CHAPTER FOUR

The yew tree's ability to maintain its dark emerald needles
year-round served, in ancient thought, as a metaphor for
immortality. Moreover, the tendency of its branches to reroot
themselves to form new, but connected, trunks illustrated
death and rebirth. Yew staves were used in pagan Ireland to
measure corpses and their graves.

—*Mystical Trees, Runes, Wands*

*I*n my memory, Austin pulls me to the center of the field. He's hitched the horse to a tree branch. He's supposed to be exercising the horse . . . Old Jerry. A lovely fawn-colored bay. Old Jerry. Just remembering the name brings a solid rush of smells, colors, emotions, sounds . . . I'm vividly lost to a self who doesn't exist anymore. The version of me, Eleanor Darrow, who loved the firm neck of Old Jerry, who brought him apples from the kitchens, cutting them in half with my apron knife upon a rock.

And how I loved the lad who tended the horses.

Austin pulls me, and his grin is like to break my heart for all its ignorance of how the world will collapse around us later.

"What think you of the view?" he asks.

"Glorious," I say.

"Indeed, lassie, indeed! And would you like it for the view as you stand in a window and look out, waiting for me?"

"What, are ye to be building me a window here in the field?" I ask.

"Aye, a window and a wall, and let's say four of them, lass!"

I remember staring at him. Those lovely ruddy cheeks, his broad face with the deep blue eyes, his sandy-colored hair in unruly curls.

"Ought I to build you a house out here in this meadow, then?" he prompts.

"This could be our home?" I ask. I laugh, and I remember that the sound, delighted and sudden, drove a rook from its station. "But why would I live here in shame with the likes of you?"

"No shame when you wear my ring and carry my name."

"But I've never been asked," I tease.

The flash of his smile then. It had all been orchestrated. He plunges to his knee in the flowers, then casts about in them for a bit until he thrusts back up a blowsy bouquet for me. I take them and sink my face into their fragrance, happy to have a place to hide my blushing cheeks. I could sauce him and then regret it, my emotions so varied back then. He made me confident, and then I became shy.

"Miss Eleanor Darrow, as you have found a place of kind affection in my heart, and as our lives should be brought together in a manner that announces our tender feelings for each other to the world such that we may not be rendered asunder and may—"

"However did you find this many words in all the world?" I ask, amazed.

"Please, I have it memorized . . . rendered asunder and may find eternal happiness in that institution so revered throughout the ages by eager lovers who . . ."

I can't help it. I laugh.

"Eleanor!" he says, thunderstruck.

"Austin, why are you talking like this?"

"I wanted it to be special. And you are laughing!"

"Did you not mean it to be . . . at least in part humorous?"

"No!" He looks incredibly indignant.

"But we never talk this way."

"We never talk this way because we never speak of such important things."

"'Tis true," I say. I put my hand to the side of his jaw. Even now I believe I can conjure up the feel of that warm skin and the rough blond whiskers that scraped my palm.

"I wish you would marry me, Eleanor," he says simply.

His eyes staring up at me. I understand photographs, the impulse to forever capture a moment and look at it whenever you like. If I could choose one instant from my entire life, the most intense and gorgeous trice, discarding all other views my eyes took in, it would be this: the look on his face, the promise between us, and behind his head stretching the green expanse of the meadow, his hair backlit by a ponderous horizon-bent sun.

Austin.

A sob escapes me.

I had forgotten why I haunted this meadow. It was the place of the most happiness I had ever been delivered.

To outwit my own emotion, I walk toward the tree where Old Jerry had been tethered that day. It's so much bigger, its expanse of overarching limbs almost the size of a house now. It makes me think of that yew tree that Phoebe told us was beneath the surface of a pond on the Arnaud estate, glowing underwater with ancient symbols, an unpleasant burden trapped in its branches.

The yew was said to be magical. The villagers a generation

before me cut it down, fearing its power, and flooded the site so the felled and impotent tree could not even be seen.

As I approach this tree, nothing more important than a bearer of acorns and a holder of horses, a feeling of unease comes over me.

Why?

I stare at its trunk. Only a few more strides will bring me to it.

I stop.

There is something awful on the other side of the trunk. Something desperately, awfully terrible.

I take a few steps backward.

I'm not ready to face what's over there.

Wishing Miles or Phoebe were here, I look around. I could probably draw them to me with intention—or better yet, get myself out of here. And yet, I need to confront my fears. I'm the girl who pulls a knife from her apron pocket to save the world . . . or at least thinks it will save the world.

I take a few steps forward and press my hand to where the tree trunk should be. I can't feel it. My hand passes through it. I make the motions of "walking" around the tree to come to the other side.

I don't know what I expect to see: a figure in black, a trap, a demon. But what I see seizes my heart instantly and brings me to my knees. I knew it was here but I couldn't let myself remember.

It's my gravestone. A small gray stone. No consecrated churchyard for me, as the stone states: ELEANOR DARROW, *Dead by her own hand.*

My mind pushes me back in time, to that terrible day when another maid told me Madame Arnaud yet lived. I knew my life was worth nothing; she'd find me and torture me far worse than anything I could do to quickly usher myself out of this life.

I did it so quickly I hardly had time to think, terrified she'd catch me first.

I didn't leave a note or say good-bye to anyone. I had no idea where Austin was. As soon as the maid had informed me, I had raced out of the manor, leaving her spluttering with her coal hod heavy in her hands.

I'd bolted down the servants' stairs to the ground floor, emerged out the kitchen yard, and ran for my life . . . ran to protect my life so that I might take it.

As I ran, Madame Arnaud might have been watching from any of those hundreds of windows, a smile toying at her lips. I'd been her lady's maid and tried to kill her in her bed. Oh, I knew she'd love to watch me suffer, so I ran, my skirts in my way, my chest hot, and my breath a fire in my throat.

I ran here.

To the meadow where a future had been promised to me, where I was to live in a cottage built by the man I loved.

It was all ruined by my own presumptuous heroism.

In that terrible gamble, I lost everything.

I called Austin's name once, knowing he could never hear me at this faraway field. I had hastened, knowing my time to be short. There was no rope on the limb; it was back in the stable with Old Jerry. I thought of climbing to the top to cast myself down, but what if I only broke my bones and lay there helpless, prey to Madame Arnaud's worse actions? I looked down at my own crisp white apron, covering me from my chest to the hem of my skirts. It was long enough, sturdy enough. I took it off and fashioned it into a rope of sorts.

I climbed onto that branch and fastened the rope, said a prayer for myself and for the protection of my family and Austin's family. Breathing heavily, I said a prayer for the children of Grenshire, for, after all, my actions had been for their gain, as useless as they turned out to be. I leaned back to see the blue sky through the broad and light-struck leaves, wanting to die with beauty on my mind. My heart never calmed, though, raced like a jackrabbit's as I lowered myself and hesitated, swinging on the strength of my arms until I lifted myself up, such that I could bite the bark with my teeth, lifted myself so that with the abrupt drop my neck would snap. I didn't want to strangle; I did it neatly so it would be quick.

Who found me and cut me down, I'll never know. I was somewhere else for that part. I do so fervently hope it wasn't Austin.

But of course it must've been.

CHAPTER FIVE

Not until 1983 was the ban lifted that prevented suicide victims from being buried in Catholic cemeteries. The prohibition was originally intended both as a denouncement of sin and as a deterrent to suicide.

—*Religion and Viewpoints on Death*

A century is quite a long time to rue one's decisions. Two centuries makes it almost unbearable to contemplate.

I might've chosen incorrectly. Perhaps I ought to have been more brave, come to Austin's family and asked their protection, magical or prosaic as it might've been. At the very least, I should have said good-bye to Austin. It's possible he never knew why I'd done it.

He probably assumed I'd killed myself just like all the other servants who had done so, for the pure shame and remorse of how the manor treated children. It makes me sad, even to this day, that he might not have ever known the sacrifice I made on their behalf.

Apparently, I was well thought of. The entire household, hundreds of serving girls and footmen and butlers and stable lads and groundskeepers, rose up and left their duties. My death was the catalyst for the manor emptying. Why mine, and not that of poor Elsie Harlow or Maud Pike or any number of servants who took their own lives?

I stare down at the words on the tombstone. Whoever

ordered its making had wanted the world to know I'd killed myself.

ELEANOR DARROW
Dead by her own hand
October 20, 1839–July 9, 1856

So, after all, my parents did mark my birthdate. They never celebrated it, but they knew it. Or at least recorded it in the family Bible so they could later include it on my grave marker.

I was born on October 20, just like Miles and Phoebe.

A gleam of pride flows through me, so recently wrecked by the awful remembrance of my suicide. So I *am* special like they are, part of the triad. I wasn't brought along simply to serve them; I'm their equal.

I look down at my apron. In death, it has refastened itself around my neck in a less fatal way. It's just part of my uniform again. It has long been the symbol of my lesser rank, and I suddenly hate its white expanse.

I undo the waist ties and pull it up over my head. I regard it. In some other incarnation, it caused my death. Now it's just a bunch of stiff fabric. I ball it up and throw it as far as I can. It's instantly swallowed by the tall grass.

Good.

I decide it's time to share what I've learned with Phoebe and Miles. I intention back to the manor.

I find them on the staircase landing in the old part of the manor. They're with that terrible fellow who doesn't know he's dead yet. I can tell from the conversation I catch midstream that he's pressed Phoebe to take him on a tour. I can see that Miles, too, is fascinated, although we've been through the manor many times now. For me, it's a dreary place. Its spectacular architecture holds no allure for me. I know it to be a place of incredible mistreatment and criminal behavior.

"Fancy having a party here!" Alexander's saying. "Put the band on the landing and the bar can be over there by that huge fireplace. We could set up some boards and the bartenders could actually fit *in* the fireplace."

"I don't think there are going to be any parties here, mate," says Miles.

"But it's your house, right?" he appeals to Phoebe.

"Not really," she says.

"Your folks go out of town, we'll rink it up," he says.

"It will require remarkable feats of physics, given your state," says Miles. He glances over at me, and I can see he's not exactly warming up to our new companion.

"Whoa! Where'd you come from?" asks Alexander. His eyes widen in surprise as he notices me, and then a grin of the most unctuous sort affixes to his face. I've always hated that expression on a man's face, and nearly two hundred years of being dead hasn't softened me.

"I was in a meadow," I say properly.

"Your apron," says Phoebe.

"I'm not going to wear it anymore," I say.

Phoebe smiles and makes some interesting gesture with her fists in the air, which I take to be encouraging.

"You could take off another layer, too," says Alexander, leering at me.

"Leave her alone," says Miles.

"Isn't your costume thing over now?" says Alexander.

"Put on your regular clothes. I want to see what you really look like."

The tone in his voice is possessive and presumptuous. How I long to put him in his place, but that has never been part of my nature.

"Seriously!" he continues. "That black thing just totally hides everything you've got going on, doesn't it?"

"Next subject, please," says Phoebe. "You know, we need to figure out what happened to you, Alexander."

"What do you mean?" he asks. "Nothing happened to me. Hey, this is a cool scene."

He's looking at the stained glass window on the landing, where the stairs split into two different directions. It's a battle scene. Two medieval knights fight each other. One is rising up with a sword, while the other is aiming down with a spear.

"Kind of like an old-school video game," he adds.

"Or old-school life," says Miles.

Alexander starts laughing, an unpleasantly high-pitched sound. "Check it out!" he says. "Look at this! It's an X-rated window!"

I have no idea what he means, but Phoebe rolls her eyes at Miles.

"I don't think they used XXX to mean that in the Middle Ages," she says.

"Well, duh! There's only dudes here! And their clothes are on. Those stupid arses."

"Alexander, you told us you were out in the woods when you saw something that scared you," says Phoebe flatly. She's uninterested in Alexander's line of thought.

"If you want to make it X-rated," says Alexander, "get

some chicks in there in those crazy dresses that push their tits up to their chin—you know the ones I mean? With the crisscrosses up the front? And then get them started."

I don't understand all that he's saying, but I do know the term *tits*, used only by the most vulgar men. I turn and begin descending the staircase. I won't stand for that kind of language in my presence.

"Wait! Oh, come on. I'm just kidding," calls Alexander. "I'm sorry!" But he ruins his apology by instantly saying to Miles in a low voice I'm not expected to hear, "But this is the one I'd really like to see in one of those outfits. Can you picture it?"

I look up at Phoebe, still on the landing. She's angry, but also half smiling, I think out of relief that I'm this man's target instead of her. "Listen," she says, "we want to hear about your woodland adventures. Who'd you see out there?"

"No clue what you're talking about," says Alexander, but I notice the lines of worry around his eyes. He doesn't want to talk about it. He's still scared.

"You got roughed up in the face," says Miles.

Alexander shrugs. "Tree branches scratched me." But as soon as he says it, his shrug turns. He leaves his shoulders up near his ears, and his face takes on a wince.

"There was someone there?" prompts Miles.

"I don't want to talk about it," says Alexander. "Do you have anything I could drink?"

"Another Sangreçu candidate," Phoebe mutters.

"There's nothing here," says Miles.

Alexander stares at all of us. I can tell he's on the verge of understanding more, of taking that vital step to knowing that he's not in the world of the living anymore.

"Screw you guys," he says. "I'm off."

And he trudges down the stairs. He's not using intention. He's trying to convince himself his body still operates like a body.

I say nothing as he passes me, but take notice of how his eyes rake down my body. Instinctively, I cross my arms across my chest. I feel exposed without my apron, although my black dress certainly provides a decent shield for lustful eyes.

We watch in silence as he exits through the main doors.

"Should we follow him?" asks Phoebe.

Miles shakes his head. "I'm starting to remember stuff about that guy. I actually knew him, sort of. He's a few years older than me and already off to university. I think he was involved in some kind of a scandal."

"For what?"

"Treating women badly." Miles says it briefly, but I know behind those three short words is a world of pain, of women who may never get their lives back on track again.

"What a creep," says Phoebe.

"Maybe we should follow at a distance," I suggest. "We don't have to talk with him, but we should see if he leads us to his grave. Which reminds me that I need to tell you something."

"You found yours?" Miles is looking at me alertly.

"I did."

"And?"

"I'm an October 20 child, just like you."

Phoebe whoops and comes to hug me. "I knew it!" she says.

Miles gives me a lopsided smile that, I have to admit, makes my heart feel lopsided as well. But Miles belongs to Phoebe. I suppress the joy his smile gives me.

"Where was it?" Miles asks.

"A beautiful meadow. It's a place I've haunted quite a bit over the last centuries. In fact, I wasn't in the manor much until you two called me to you."

"Any other clues on the stone? Did you have the same emblem Austin has?"

I shake my head. "No. But . . ."

They both wait.

"There's a reason I'm not in the churchyard with all my family," I say. "That's hallowed ground, not permitted for sinners like me."

Phoebe frowns, but Miles understands instantly. I can tell by the look on his face. "So many others did that," he says gently.

I nod. "I know. It was practically an epidemic at one time. The Arnaud Servants Disease."

"I'm sorry," says Phoebe. She rubs her hand up and down my arm. I bristle a little and step back. Once again, a void opens between us. She and Miles both had lovely lives from what I can tell, with parents who loved them, and comfortable living with enough food to eat. They attended school rather than blacking someone's hearth with hands so cold I had to blow on them. They were snatched away from their lives, not by choice. Not like me. The manner of my death is another one of those profound differences between us.

"It's all right," I say, but I know my tone is cold. I turn away. "I think I'd like to visit the stables. So many memories of Austin are rising up."

Phoebe says, "Of course," in a small, hurt voice.

"Be safe," says Miles. "Come back instantly if something seems amiss."

"I will," I say.

I use intention to move to the stables, the dust-drifted barn from where even the horses abandoned the manor. Their stall doors are left ajar. There's some rotted hay left in Old Jerry's bin, as I wander into his close quarters to look. Harness and gear still on the wall pegs.

This was the place where Austin worked his magic, soothing the wildness out of the beasts, picking thorns from their frogs, and currying the lather out of their coats. He spoke to them in a voice they liked and responded to, nickering lightly as he did his tasks. I liked watching him at it, his clean white shirt growing translucent with sweat as he worked, his lips full and lush with a whistle for the commands.

I can almost picture him, bending with his rake to clean the stalls, always in motion, a handsome, vital boy who had turned into a man as I knew him. He would punch the ice atop the horses' water for them on bright cold mornings, and heave the rim against the wall to dash it. It never bothered the horses. They knew his routines. He was an apple bringer and a firm rider whose horses never dared ignore his orders. Sometimes the sight of him coming into the yard from a long ride at a gallop: oh, it could take my heart away. Austin was handsome, so unbelievably open faced and good.

I walk around, looking for some sign, something of his existence on this earth so long ago. I climb the ladder to the hayloft. We kissed here once, but it was too dangerous, too much coming and going, and I didn't want to get caught on the ladder with my reputation forever ruined.

I climb it now, a mere pretense, since intention could bring me to the top instantly. But I like imagining I feel the rungs under my palms, imagining Austin is at the bottom waiting for me to reach the hayloft before he begins climbing, such a gentleman, as it wouldn't do to have him below my skirts.

Up in the hayloft, dust is heavy. No sign of him or anyone. No dragon emblems, no secret notes left for me. Bales of hay have turned gray in the years they've sat here fermenting.

"Hey," says a voice behind me, and I jump.

I whirl around. It's Alexander, his head cresting the floor as he steps from the ladder onto the hayloft.

"What are you doing here?" he asks.

"Just looking," I say. "Actually, I was just about to go."

"Don't go," he says. "We should talk."

"Oh, I think I must be on my way, but thank you all the same," I say. The same words I've said many a time when alive, when men plucked at my skirts and tried to tarry with me.

"You're gorgeous," he says. "I'm dying to see you with your hair out of that awful braid. You're taking your job a little too seriously."

He reaches out and touches it, an appalling intimacy that I cannot countenance. I step backward, but he doesn't let go.

"Ouch!"

"And that dress . . . my God. People back then had no appreciation for a woman's body."

"Let go of my hair!"

Instead, he pulls harder, and I stumble toward him. "Let go of me!" I scream.

"Oh, I don't think so," he says. "I'm enjoying this too much."

Panic rises in me. This is not a good person. His mouth descends on mine, and I taste the bitterness of death on his tongue, fear and tree bark and terror. I twist away from him and he presses closer.

I yank my head sideways, despite the fact he has my braid captured, and elbow him as hard as I can. But it has no impact, and he tightens his other arm around my shoulders. I'm trapped.

"No, no," I try to scream, but his mouth is on mine and I can't.

Then I remember what horror has made me forget. I can be anywhere, instantly. I look into his wide, angry eyes and bring myself to Miles.

He and Phoebe are hanging out with her family. Tabby's watching a show on the television, dressed in her pajamas, and her parents are reading different sections of the newspaper.

I arrive with a shriek. Miles is instantly at my side, hands on my shoulders in a comforting grip. "Are you all right?" he asks, wide-eyed.

Phoebe races to me as well. I can see through their reaction how very upset I must appear, but Phoebe's family is unaware of the drama unfolding right before their unseeing eyes.

"It's Alexander," I say. "He cornered me in the stables."

Phoebe catches my gaze in a sisterly solidarity. Every female knows what it's like to be in that spot at some time.

"We're going right back there," says Miles firmly.

I'm about to resist, so happy to be safe, but realize we do need to take care of Alexander. He's just one of those ghosts who need to come to grips with his being dead. Then: he'll disappear. Problem solved.

"All right," I murmur.

"Take us there," says Miles.

Alexander's already down from the hayloft when we arrive, standing by one of the horse stalls.

"Hey, dick boy," says Phoebe. "You mess with her again and we'll do worse to you than what happened in the woods."

He turns a terrified gaze to us. There are three of us and only one of him.

"I didn't mean anything by it," he says.

"When a woman resists your attentions, you don't press her," I say.

"You weren't resisting too hard," he says, with a half smile aimed at Miles. He's trying to enlist Miles to his side, males against females.

"Listen, and listen well," says Miles in a low voice. "If a woman is anything other than completely willing, you back off. I know you got into trouble at university for this, and you're lucky you didn't get jail time."

Alexander rolls his eyes. He's transitioning from terror to more confidence. He's no longer on the defensive, happily taking to the offensive side and the security it offers. "Please," he says. "Do I need an engraved invitation?"

"Pretty much," says Miles.

"We were being gentle with you before, but now you get the smackdown," says Phoebe. "Don't touch Eleanor ever again. And just in case it hasn't dawned on you: you're dead."

"I know, I know," he says. "I'm officially backing off." He throws me a glance of hidden rage.

"I mean that literally," says Phoebe. "You're dead. You died. Whatever happened to you in the forest: it was permanent."

Despite everything, I do feel a hair of compassion for him as he digests her words.

"I died?" he echoes.

"It's a sad truth," I say, "and not easily absorbed. But it's why I'm able to disappear, how I evaded you."

"You're . . . ?"

"Yes, we're all three of us dead," says Miles. "Welcome to Ghost Town. Check it out."

He walks over to the stall door and kicks it. His leg goes right through the wood. Next he leaps, his whole body moving effortlessly through the door.

"See?" says Miles to Alexander.

"Oh shite," says Alexander. His face becomes gray and his eyes fill with tears. "I'm done?"

None of us answer.

"So, it's important that you tell us where your body is," says Miles. "You can move on to your heavenly reward, and we'll figure out what happened to you."

"And fix it," says Phoebe. Alexander's face responds with bright but flawed hope. "No, I mean, we'll fix it so no one *else* gets hurts," she says quickly. "We can't fix what happened to you."

"I don't know," says Alexander slowly. "I just don't . . . can't . . . I don't . . ."

"Spit it out," says Phoebe.

"You lot are bonkers," he says. "Effing liars! Screw you and your stupid games." He's about to storm out, and Miles grabs him by the sleeve.

"You're banished," he says, "until you can tell us where your body is."

"Banished? You're over the top, you effin' toffer."

"I command it," says Miles.

And just like that, Alexander is gone. I inhale and look at Miles with narrowed eyes.

"The last time you used that word *command*," says Phoebe, "it worked like a charm. I think you should use it more often."

"It does seem to have some power," says Miles grimly.

I hadn't heard about this before. When and where did he wield such a word? Perhaps at Versailles when he and Phoebe were battling Giraude? Sensations wash over me.

We didn't always have these bodies, these identities. Miles used to be someone who made commands, it seems. And Phoebe is someone who betrayed me. Who was I? Someone who fought with swords, along with Miles. It's all bewildering and strange, and I crave answers. We are all connected by our birth dates and the fact we have not moved on to the other realm despite admitting we are dead. We have some task to accomplish, and it seems to have something to do with a prophecy Steven read in a book about secret societies. That's all I know . . . and it isn't enough.

CHAPTER SIX

According to a charming anecdote of Xerxes the Great, he
made soldiers whip the Hellespont River with three hundred
strokes in retaliation for a bridge coming down in a storm.
They also threw fetters into the strait, presumably trusting the
water would enchain itself. The bridge cables had been made
of flax and papyrus, so perhaps it was not the river's fault.

—*Crazy Kings & Manic Monarchs*

Steven has promised Phoebe that he would help us with researching the prophecy and what our job here on this earth might entail. Each night he leaves out a book on the kitchen table, open to a page that might help us. Each morning it is our habit to look at what he left out for us.

Today's offering is nonsense. Something about snow worship. "I guess this is the root of the fear about the abominable snowman," says Phoebe.

"What is that?" I ask.

"So not even worth asking about. It's like Steven is joking with us," says Miles.

So we move on to do our own looking. The manor library is a glorious collection of books, three stories' worth, accessed by slim walkways and moving staircases. I had adopted a small chamber for myself long ago, up under the rafters. I had fancied the comfort of the books, although they only turned their spines toward me. I liked being separate from the other maids, since we were all made morose by our guilt. Here in my tiny room, hardly big enough to hold a cot, I could nurse my pain to myself.

Phoebe, the only one of us who can touch the Arnaud furnishings, pulls a book off the shelf; its spine reads *Greco-Roman Cults*. It has gilt page edges and an odor that exudes from the time-pressed fibers. She turns pages carefully and stops on a page about an ancient cult that worshipped the moon.

"This may seem far-fetched," she says, "but when I was newly Sangreçu and told Mom and Steven that Miles and I have the same birthday, Steven said he thought maybe moon phases have something to do with our situation."

I lean over and study the two facing pages, smiling to myself at the woodcut engraving of a woman wearing a crescent moon on her head.

The chapter is broken up, and as I look at its heading, something stirs in me. I point to the heading *Chapter IX*.

"This looks like the writing on the stained glass window," I say.

Phoebe gasps. "Oh my God," she says. "It never occurred to me. Those are Roman numerals."

"The window says *thirty*," says Miles. We all look at each other. "Does that help?" he adds plaintively.

"Is there a cult that worshipped the number thirty? Like a trinity, but based on tens?" asks Phoebe.

I drop my head to my hands. It's ridiculous. No one builds a church around numbers. We are grasping at straws.

"Well, it does mean something," insists Phoebe. "I can't believe those *X*'s are for the letter—there aren't enough words that begin with *X*."

"It's an olden days X-ray cult," jokes Miles.

"Weren't there ancient Greeks whose names started with *X*? Like Xerxes?"

"Who?" ask Miles and Phoebe at the same time.

I smile. There is so much about the modern world I don't know—but it seems my curriculum, truncated though it was, included a primer on the ancient world that isn't offered to students nowadays.

"He was a Persian king," I inform them. "From the period before Christ."

"Do you think he could have followers to this day?" asks Phoebe.

"Possibly," I say. "I don't really recall much about him."

"Were there other famous people whose name started with *X*? Maybe there were three of them, to explain the three *X*'s. Xerxes and two others," says Miles.

"I have to admit, I can't think of a single one."

"So it's repeated for emphasis," says Phoebe. "Xerxes, Xerxes, Xerxes!" She walks away laughing, goes to look through the books. It's a needle-in-a-haystack search, but maybe someday the right book's spine will call to her.

After spending the morning wandering the stacks, we return to Phoebe's family. Tabby's taking her nap, we confirm as we check on her asleep in her crib. Sweetly enough, her mum slumbers in the chair in her room as well, a book slumped onto the floor. She must've fallen asleep reading to her.

The doorbell rings but neither she nor Tabby wakes up.

We go to see who it is. Steven opens the door only a crack.

"Hullo," says a friendly but awkward male voice. Miles makes a harsh sound in his throat. "We're Mr. and Mrs. Whittleby. I wonder . . . do you know of us?"

"I'm afraid not," says Steven neutrally. He doesn't open the door any wider.

"Well, this is all quite a bit strange. Our son is Miles. He's no longer with us. He passed on, and I understand your daughter passed on as well."

Steven doesn't answer.

A woman's voice breaks in. "It's terrible to talk so abruptly of such a raw topic, I'm sure. I apologize. The thing is, our son . . . well, he . . . returned to us."

Miles's face is a study of anguish, and I can barely look at him. In turn, he can't take his eyes off his parents. He's blazing with the desire to be seen by them.

"He told us to come talk to you," says the man.

"Why doesn't he open the door and invite them in?" asks Phoebe.

"It is a painful topic," says Steven.

"Did your daughter return to you?" the man presses.

"Too painful," says Steven. "I'm sorry."

He eases the door closed as the man says, "Well, now!" and the woman shrieks out a rushed "I'm so very sorry!"

Steven rests his forehead against the door and breaks into loud sobs.

"Why won't he *talk* to them?" Phoebe wails. "Open the door, Steven!"

"My poor parents," says Miles. He glares at Steven's back and balls his hands into fists.

"Are you okay, Miles?" Phoebe asks.

"I'll be back later." He vanishes.

"I can't believe this," says Phoebe. "Why wouldn't he let them in?"

Steven cries for so long that Phoebe's frustration turns to sorrow for him. I comfort her as she cries, too. "Maybe he can talk to them later," she says. "When he's calmed down."

"Of course," I say soothingly. "They've made the first step, and it's his turn to call on them when he's ready."

Finally, Steven wipes his eyes on his shirtsleeve and staggers to the living room. He turns on the telly.

It's the middle of a news broadcast. I bite my lip as I see that Alexander's disappearance is the top news. A large photo of him is shown behind the newsman's desk as he describes all the efforts being taken to find him. It seems Alexander was last seen in his university city of Exeter, so search efforts are concentrated there. His mother and father, Grenshire residents, are briefly seen in footage as they move, distracted in their grief, from the police station into a waiting car.

"Gosh, they haven't found him yet?"

Startled, I whip my head around.

It's a new girl. She's modern, dressed in calf-length boots and a belted dress. Her face is scratched like Alexander's, but not to the same degree. It looks as if she didn't struggle as hard, perhaps.

She looks at me with a bit of a frown—maybe I should think seriously about adopting the clothing of today, but I have no idea how to make that happen, and I don't think Phoebe can just hand me over a sweater—and quickly glances over at Phoebe with a more relaxed face. "I would've thought they'd find him by now," she said.

"What's your name?" Phoebe asks.

"Oh, hey, I'm Dee," she says. "Can you believe the manor has a telly inside it?"

Miles returns just then, and I watch to see if Dee reacts to his sudden appearance. She looks down at the ground. It's as if she's coaching her mind not to take in anything that contradicts the idea that she's alive.

"They're beside themselves," Miles says. "Wish I'd never told them to come see your bleeding parents." His face is flushed red with anger. He doesn't seem to have noticed Dee.

"Did you know Alexander very well?" Phoebe asks Dee, ignoring Miles.

"No," says Dee. "I guess he went to Emmons School like me, but I didn't know him. Do you go to Emmons?"

"No," says Phoebe, "but Miles here did." She points to Miles, and I watch the girl's face transform from open interest to horror.

"Miles Whittleby?" the girl says. She waves her arms around like she's on an edge about to fall off backward.

"That's me," he says. "Or was."

"You were in that accident," she says.

"That's right."

"But they said you . . . *died.* But you didn't die."

"They were correct," says Miles. "I did die."

"But *no,*" she says. "It's not possible."

I look away as she rapidly reviews the information presented to her before her very eyes, as she comes to understand that if she can see him, she is *like* him.

"Do you know what happened to you?" I ask in a hushed voice when I've judged enough time has gone by.

She's quietly crying by the time I look back. "I just wanted to see what was going on at the manor," she says. "I heard my mum saying there was trouble here. They'd found something in the ground."

"Swords," says Phoebe.

"Yes, that's right. And I thought I'd like to get a look."

"And then?" asks Phoebe.

"It was all over so quickly," she says, wiping away at her tears, with fresh ones taking their place.

"Were you scared?"

She doesn't bother to answer but keeps quietly crying.

"We're trying to solve things," says Miles. "Anything you can tell us could help. Do you remember what happened?"

"One minute I was walking along that pretty path in the

woods. And I was thinking how glad I was that such a nice path existed. And then . . ."

"What?"

"I've got to get out of here," she says. "Do you know how I can call my mum? Can I borrow your phone? She won't pick up when I call her."

"I know it's hard to think about what happened," says Phoebe, "but you've got to talk about it. Tell us so we can help you."

She gives Phoebe a long, long look. "I don't know if there is anything that can be helped anymore."

Phoebe nods. "It's true," she says frankly.

"Am I . . . like you?" Dee asks Miles.

"I'm afraid so," he says.

"So does my mum know yet?"

"We don't know," he says. "You can . . . you can go look at her, you know. You just think of her and you can be there. But please don't go until you tell us what happened to you."

"Well . . ." she says. "I just want to go home."

"Okay, just, maybe one thing. Can you tell us if it was one person who harmed you? Or several?"

"There was no one to stop it happening." She crosses her arms and looks cold suddenly. She's in shock.

"What did they look like?" I ask her. "Like me? Old-fashioned clothing?"

"I was so scared," she says.

I can see Phoebe visibly give up. "Well, I think they got Alexander, too," she says, pointing to the TV screen, where the story on his disappearance is being updated by a few words from a police officer.

"Why did I ever come?" the girl asks herself. "I should've stayed home."

"It's not your fault," says Miles.

"Thank you," she says. "But I deserve it. There are signs everywhere warning to stay out of the woods. I ignored them."

"Everyone does," says Miles. "You don't need to beat yourself up over it. You were just out on a lark, seeing what you could see."

"Yes, that's right," she says. "I wish I hadn't gone alone, though. Maybe it wouldn't have happened if I wasn't alone."

"And how did they hurt you?" Phoebe asks again. We have to know. It feels terrible to be probing her in this way, but if it helps us figure things out, it's worth it.

"I don't want to talk about it."

"Can you at least tell us *where* it happened?"

Dee shakes her head.

"Can you take us there?"

"No," says Dee, and she begins crying again. "I've got to go," she says. And just like that, she does.

"Not good," says Miles. "What's going on?"

We all jolt as the doorbell rings again. Steven swears from his armchair, and in reaction Miles looks like he's going to punch him.

"If he doesn't let them in this time, I'm going to . . ." he threatens.

"Going to what?" asks Phoebe. "Waft through him?"

This time the doorbell has woken Phoebe's mum and Tabby, and they join Steven at the door.

It's not Miles's parents.

It's two police officers. There's no question that Steven has to open the door now. They come into the foyer and their eyes immediately flit all around. They, like everyone else in Grenshire, are curious about the interior of the Arnaud Manor.

"Good afternoon," says one of them. "Are you Steven Arnaud?"

"I am."

"I'd like to sit down with you and ask you a few questions," says the officer.

"What is this about?"

"We'll discuss that once we're situated. I'll talk to you separately, ma'am," he says to Phoebe's mother.

She tightens her grip on Tabby, and I see the wild look in her eyes. She's *done* with trouble and danger.

"Is this about those stupid swords?" she says. "It's our land; it's our right to dig. We've called in the proper archeological people to assess the find and we'll comply with their directions."

"It's not about the swords," says the officer dismissively. "I need a place to sit down with you where we can talk privately. Officer Huddleston will stay with you, ma'am, while we talk."

"But . . ." says Phoebe's mum.

"We'll do as you say, officers," says Steven.

"This is official police business," says Officer Huddleston. "You're obliged to comply." Without asking for any further permission, he steps around Steven, his hand on his billy club as if someone's going to jump out at him at any minute.

"Someone stay with Mom," says Phoebe. "I want to hear what the other one asks Steven."

Without even thinking about it, my feet carry me over to Phoebe, and therefore Miles is left behind with Phoebe's mum, Tabby, and Officer Huddleston. The other officer, who introduces himself as Officer Stonecroft, keeps step with Steven as he ushers him into the den.

"Take a seat," says Steven. There's no other chair in the room other than the one at his desk, so he leans sideways against the wall and crosses his arms. Without a word, Officer Stonecroft swiftly walks back to the dining room and hoists one of the chairs as if it were a feather, bringing it back to the den and parking it in front of Steven.

"Sit," he says.

With a sigh, Steven does so.

"Tell me about last night," says the officer.

"Not much to tell. We had dinner and put our child to bed. We talked a little, watched one show, and went to bed ourselves."

"At what time?"

Steven shrugs. "Maybe ten?"

"Who else did you talk to?"

"Just my wife and child."

"Anyone come to the door?"

Steven frowns. "No."

"Did you go outside yourself last night?"

"No."

"Your wife?"

"No."

"Make any phone calls?"

"No. Look, can you tell me what this is all about?"

"I'm asking the questions here," says Officer Stonecroft. Steven's face tightens. "You and your wife saw no one but your child, and thus you vouch for each other's presence here at home all night."

"That's right," says Steven.

"Tell me a little about yourself," invites the officer.

"Seriously?"

The officer gives him a narrow-lidded look.

"Let's see. I'm forty-six years old, born here but raised in the United States. I'm a software engineer. I have two children but only one survives."

Officer Stonecroft suddenly looks alert. "What happened to the other child?"

"She died in a drowning accident while we still lived in California."

"When was this?"

"Last year."

"And you moved to Grenshire just a bit ago."

I see how it looks to the officer. If there was anything suspicious about Phoebe's death, it looks like her parents fled the country. And it's dawning on me that Steven's being questioned about Alexander . . . and possibly Dee.

"We wanted a fresh start. And this house had been on the market for so many years with no takers. It seemed like a good way to give our youngest daughter a second start. All of us, really."

"You are Steven Arnaud."

"That's right."

"Did you go by any other name in the States?"

"No."

"So if I placed a call to that jurisdiction, they could confirm your address in . . . ?"

"San Francisco. Yes."

"Please write it down here," says Officer Stonecroft.

As I drift back to check on Phoebe's mum, Officer Stone-croft continues to ask questions of Steven: if he has a criminal record, if he has ever gone under any other name. I can tell he's using a barrage of questions to try to get Steven to misspeak, to make a mistake and say something incriminating. How awful, after everything this family has been through, that he is now under suspicion of murder.

In the dining room, I see that Phoebe's mum is also suffering under an onslaught of questions. "We were both here all night," she's saying as I arrive.

"Are you a light sleeper?"

"I tend to be."

"Is it possible your husband could've slipped out at night and you wouldn't have noticed?"

She draws herself up at that and glares at Officer Huddleston. "My husband doesn't 'slip out' at night."

"Two children have gone missing," says Officer Huddleston. "Both Grenshire teenagers. One of them told her friends she was going to see the artifacts that had been discovered. She never came home."

Phoebe's mum gasps. "So that boy we were seeing on the news . . . he's not the only one missing?"

"That's right." Officer Huddleston lowers his voice and leans in toward her, as if he is sharing a confession. "We need your help. Two mothers are missing their children tonight. You can imagine how that feels. If you know anything, please tell us."

She reacts as if she'd been slapped. "I feel for both the mothers *and* the fathers," she says. "You don't even know how much I can feel for them. I have been there and experienced it to the degree that no parent should have to endure. But if you are insinuating—and I believe you are—that my husband had anything to do with those missing children, you are dead wrong."

"I didn't mean to insinuate that," he says, although clearly that is what he meant. "We're duty-bound to investigate. The last place this young woman spoke of going happens to be land your house sits on. We have to ask. It's uncomfortable, but we have to do it."

She doesn't respond, but hatred and misery blare out of her eyes. I'm wondering how much of the officer's investigation is based on Dee's statement to a friend that she was coming here and how much has to do with the historic legend of this house, a place where, over centuries, many, many children have disappeared. It hasn't happened for a long time, but it seems coincidental, I can see from his view, that soon after Steven and his family have taken over residence at the manor, the disappearances have started up again.

"Has your husband seemed changed since you moved here?" he asks.

I see the struggle on her face. She wants to say, *Of course he's changed, we lost our daughter*, but that would open up a terrible line of questioning, so she simply shakes her head.

"Sure about that?" he asks.

"I'm sure."

"I want you to think of me as a friend," he says. "I know you care about these missing children. You're a mother. I want to find them, and you do, too. If you can help me, call me." He gives her a card.

"Appalling sexism on your part," she flares at him. "Maybe I'm the one with the kids in the dungeon, and he's the one you should be handing the card to."

"Oh shite, lady, shut it," breathes Miles, and we exchange a pained glance.

"Maybe you haven't seen the statistics," says the officer unconcernedly. "It's rarely women, and almost always men." He stands up and starts walking down the hallway to the den, where Steven's still talking with Officer Stonecroft.

Maybe, after all, he hasn't heard of Madame Arnaud?

CHAPTER SEVEN

How fascinating to consider the boatloads of three Germanic
tribes, the Angles, Saxons, and Jutes, who settled in the
Roman province Britannia to found their own civilization,
and, thankfully to those of us who speak it, a new language.
Ah, to have been the king of Kent in 597 when Pope Gregory's
curious delegation arrived to find the tribes now organized as
kingdoms, all under his rule!

—*History of Our English Tongue*

*A*fter the officers leave, Phoebe's parents naturally begin a litany of comparing notes with each other. "They suspect you're behind that boy's disappearance," says Phoebe's mother. "And there's a girl missing now, too."

Steven frowns. "He didn't tell me that."

"Probably hoping you'd slip up and say something about her."

Steven sinks to a chair at the dining room table, putting his head in his hands. "I'm tired of all this. It's not worth fighting. They don't want us here at the manor, and now we're suspects in missing child cases? I know we wanted some distraction when we moved to England, but this is more than I bargained for."

"We're not giving up," says Phoebe's mother firmly. "Phoebe's doing something, with Miles and that other girl she spoke of. We have to stay here until they can figure out their task."

"But if I wind up in prison?"

"That's not going to happen."

"I hate this," says Phoebe. "What if they really do think

Steven's behind this? Not just investigating but truly operating under some erroneous belief that he came to England to abduct kids?"

"They're casting about for any explanation," says Miles. "Of course they had to interview him; Dee told her friend she was coming here, and they never saw her again."

I look down at my front, so newly black. I'm used to the gleam of white from my apron. I feel like a bloated crow, sick with seed. "Phoebe and Miles, would you mind if I take myself away for a bit?"

Phoebe looks stricken. "Of course. I'm sorry for what you learned yesterday."

I shrug. "It turns out I was the same as any other servant here. I took the coward's way out."

"You thought she was going to torture you," Miles reminds me. "You wanted a quick, easy death, not to spend years as her captive."

In a way, I *have* spent years as a captive, haunting the Arnaud Manor and the meadow. But at least physical pain was removed from the equation.

I smile at them and intention myself onto the front courtyard of the manor. I look up at the façade of the home, so many mullioned windows and gables, a profusion of stone against the twilit sky. I have no idea where to go, but I know I need to be alone with my thoughts.

The meadow is no longer a peaceful place for me . . . at least, not for a while.

I decide to go to Austin's cottage, where his family once embraced me as a member. I can look at the emblem on the door again, the same as on Austin's tombstone.

It's a nice walk from the manor so I elect to do it as the living do, foot by foot, although that is only an illusion for me. A pleasant footpath, largely overgrown, leads up to a cart path along a hedgerow, and it is this I follow as darkness begins to fall.

His cottage stops me right in my tracks.

I thought it would be moss and ivy covered, lost to the creep of the forest's claiming of the rocks that formed it . . . But instead its windows gleam with light. There are people moving around inside. A gentle peaty smoke drifts from the chimney.

I pause at the door to look at the emblem, studying the monster's face. Phoebe and Miles call it a dragon but that's not exactly right. It's got a human aspect somehow. Its visage feels expressive of emotion in a way only a human's could. He is howling at his imprisonment.

I pity him.

I feel a rush of disgust and anger at his treatment. My fingernails long to dig into the wood, but I have no ability. I'm as helpless as the trapped beast.

I enter the cottage and clap my hands to my mouth in shock.

Where Austin's family once had a modest collection of benches at the table and a chair by the fire, the house is now handsomely and modernly furnished. Overstuffed chairs provide a comfort that Mrs. Fairecloth's simple cushions never could have. The lighting is warm; electric lights provide a brightness the candles and kerosene lamps weren't capable of. It's Austin's home but rendered in completely different flavoring. It's as if someone took a book I loved and bound it differently, using a wildly different typeface.

And: there are people here. Not Austin's family, but perhaps they are familial descendants. Reginald Boswick is here, which shocks me. Is this his home now? Is that why the symbol figures on his business card—only that, and nothing more? Just a curiosity?

He is joined by another man and woman, roughly his age, and a teenage girl. I focus on her as she is the one talking as I enter.

"I *saw* him," she says. "We know he died, but he was before me as real as the living."

"It's simply not possible, my dear. Your eyes deceived you," says the older woman, whose gray hair is in a bun.

The girl makes an annoyed noise and pushes her dark hair behind her ears. "I was in his house," she says. "And I saw him. Who else would I have seen there?"

I frown. I think that . . . she's talking about Miles. After he drank the Sangreçu blood, he temporarily gained corporeality. He told Phoebe and me he'd seen a girl our age visiting his parents. I believe this must be her.

"But surely you are mistaken. We attended the funeral. The lad is dead and in the ground."

"I came down the stairs and found him with his parents. It was a chaotic scene. He was trying to calm down his mother and simultaneously tell them about someone else, a girl at the Arnaud Manor."

"The child? The girl they call Tabitha?"

"I don't know. He didn't say her name. He disappeared in the midst of talking to them. He was there, paler and paler, as if my eyes were blurring, and then gone."

"That is strange beyond belief," says Boswick.

"Do you believe he could have . . . ?" murmurs the man.

"No," says the woman firmly. "It is simply impossible. The dead do not drink."

"But how else to explain his sudden appearance to his family?"

"Tell us everything he said, Raven," he appeals to the girl, and by his naming her, I realize she is indeed the one Miles spoke of.

"He said the manor had a family living in it, and he met their daughter, and he wanted his parents to work with the parents. He said there was magic there."

"So then perhaps there *is* something to this family's line."

"I'd hoped so, given the fact the family has been tracked for centuries. But when he died we had simply lost hope."

"The threads we follow are thin indeed," says Boswick.

"Filigree," says the woman.

Silence falls among them. "Any other items to discuss?" Boswick asks.

"The swords," says the man.

"And what are we to do with that?" asks the woman.

The others rest, blank faced.

"We can't very well cover them back up, can we?"

"It's an opportunity," says Raven. "Through their discovery, we may learn more about the prophecy."

"Along with the rest of the world."

"And is that so bad?"

"It is if their mission contradicts ours."

"Forget the swords; our bigger problem is that two people have disappeared on the grounds of the manor."

"Related to our work?"

"I think not. But possibly."

"And again: What can we do?"

"Patrol the woods. Keep people out."

"Rebuild the wall blocking the driveway, shall we? And wall in that despicable new family?" the woman offers with a wry smile.

"It would serve them right," says Boswick grimly.

"Is there anything we can do to find the missing? Do we think they're . . . dead?" asks Raven.

"Of course they're dead," says Boswick. "Something has happened at the manor. A shift in power."

"I feel helpless," says Raven. "I wish I could have grabbed Miles when I saw him and brought him straight here."

"We should've spoken to him while he yet lived," says Boswick.

"We weren't to talk to him until he turned eighteen, and no one could've predicted his death," the woman reminds him.

"Sometimes our own laws hamper our progress."

"And isn't that the way of the world," she says philosophically. "Now then. We would typically have our reading of the prophecy and then adjourn for another year. But there are so many things going on. I believe we should meet back here in a week."

"Sooner," says Raven. "Things are happening. But I can't stay at the Whittleby home. Too dire for my taste. My parents will murder me if I miss more school, too. How about meeting here the day after tomorrow?"

"Indeed," says the woman approvingly. "You mustn't miss school for the sake of two silly teens who can't listen to everything their body is telling them and stay out of the woods."

"Maybe their guts didn't warn them," says Raven. "Not everyone feels the premonitions of danger."

"But *these* woods . . . !" she says, and everyone nods, eventually even Raven.

"All right, then. The official reading," says Boswick. He unrolls a scroll that is made of soft, buttery leather.

He clears his throat and begins. "'On a stronde the king

doth slumber, and below the mede the dragon bataille'—I've never known how to pronounce that," he says.

"No one here will correct you," says the woman. "Each year I feel I understand it less, rather than more."

I've heard this language before. I try hard to remember. I have a vague memory of Steven reading it aloud on the train in France. He must've read it from a book—and here's the original scroll.

". . . 'the dragon bataille the wicked brike with bisemare from yon damosel, and the goodnesse undone for she who bitrayseth. But an thee seche they of the ilke lykenes and lygnage, for a long tyme abide thee to come thereby the thre wyghts borne on the day of swich clamor for the kynge and han them drink of Sangreçu blood, then they may leere the halkes and lede the lorn to might, eftsoone do Brytayne arise to her gloire.' Very clumsily done, I'm afraid."

"Not at all," says the man. "You sound impressively authentic."

I stare down at the prophecy, burned onto the calfskin, resting on the table and curling at the edges. I wish we had known before that it was an important prophecy. How ironic that Steven just read a bit of it to us and none of us understood its significance. Or if Miles and Phoebe knew, they never told me.

The words mean little to me. I believe they are Old English. I do note that three "wyghts" are born on the day . . . just as Miles, Phoebe, and I are children of October 20. We must be the three wyghts. What on earth does that mean?

I study the end of the prophecy, where the long sentence comes to a close. We must "leere the halkes and lede the lorn to might."

The word *leere* makes me think of *leery*, so perhaps it is the root of that familiar word to me. Thus, we must beware of the halkes . . . do they mean hawks? It would be wonderful to learn exactly what we are to be afraid of. Perhaps it is the halkes that have killed Alexander and Dee in the woods.

There was no danger in the woods until recently. Over the years since the manor had been abandoned, children had come and peered in the windows, sometimes penetrated into the interior, but nothing in the woods had halted their progress.

I peer down at the ancient words, trying to sort through my thoughts. The biggest change has been Phoebe's family moving into the manor. But in the time that followed, there were no disappearances. Was it the discovery of the swords or something else? Certainly the swords *brought* Dee and Alexander to the property, but was it also the genesis of the malevolent forces that wished them harm?

"Each year, I feel at a loss," says the woman. "I will die before we see the prophecy enacted."

"We must take the long view," says Boswick. "Think of the medieval craftspeople who built the Gothic cathedrals over hundreds of years. They died with the walls half up, knowing it would be their children or even their grandchildren who would see it to completion."

"It's difficult to feel any sense of urgency when we don't even know if we'll get to see the prophecy enacted."

"But there *is* great urgency all of a sudden!" says Raven. "Miles somehow returned from the dead or never died . . . and swords were unearthed at the property!"

"And there is urgency in making sure the family there doesn't blunder and ruin everything we've built up and sustained," adds Boswick. "If they find the dragon fighter before we do, they will desecrate the site. It must be done correctly, by the correct persons. I believe we are very close to finding mirth and—"

"Yes," Raven interrupts.

Mirth and what? Whatever does laughter have to do with any of this? Seems to me that not one of these folks has had a smile grace their visage on a consistent schedule.

More troubling is the idea that we could muddle things by not doing it correctly. How are we supposed to fulfill the prophecy when we don't even understand it?

CHAPTER EIGHT

A tiny girl arrived today. All the servants sick about it.
We are complicit.

—From the diary of Eleanor Darrow

*T*he next day, I return to my chamber hidden behind the shelves in the library of the Arnaud Manor, the space where I hid from the guilt and terror of the household. Moonlight sits behind the glass where I engraved in the window *poor little babes* so many years ago.

I was so young then, etching into the glass and almost wishing it would break, that some release would come from a shard impaling my wrist. I was full of pity but didn't have enough fire to take action to change things for those children . . . and then when I did take action I failed.

I look the same now. My body is still fit and strong and my hair dark, but my mind is ancient. I look around the small room. How much has changed, and yet how little has. Why am I still around?

I wish I had been able to drink the Sangreçu blood, too. Why was Phoebe so selfish? She robbed me of the only chance to feel my own skin again. I sink onto the bed, as if I'm really on it, my head in my hands. The inky vapor of despair washes over me and tangles in my hair. I give up. I'm one of the poor little babes, too.

Slowly, voices down below drift into my consciousness. There are two men in the library. I intention back out onto the balcony and look down. It's Steven and a man I don't recognize.

"I'm eager to get the library inventoried," says Steven, "and to attach a dollar amount to its worth."

"Indeed," says the man. "And perhaps you'll find another astonishing volume, like the Louis XIV diary."

Steven smiles. "That was extraordinary, and probably not to be topped."

"Show me where that book came from," says the man, and Steven obligingly brings him over to the area.

"On this shelf here," says Steven.

"Amazing," the man says. "Do you think I could bring in a camera crew to film where the book was located? Might be a fun sort of things for the bookish to watch."

"I don't think so," says Steven. "We need to keep things quiet around here."

"And why would that be?"

"You don't know?"

"No."

Steven sighs and rubs his forehead with one hand. "Two area children have disappeared. I had even thought about canceling our appointment. I was glad you had contacted me, though, and you did sound so busy, I thought it best to keep it."

"Well, well," says the man. "Swords, books, so many wonderful things previously lost to the world have shown up here. Perhaps the children will, too."

Steven's head swiftly comes up, and he stares at the man with intensity.

"What the hell do you mean by that?"

"It's just curious that teens have *disappeared*, just as you and your family have *appeared*."

"Get out," says Steven in a rough voice. He walks to the door, but the man doesn't follow.

"Did you know those kids?" the man asks.

"I don't know them," says Steven. "Get out."

"Relieved to hear you use the present tense. They're yet alive, we all hope. Perhaps kept somewhere on the property? This is a very large manor."

Steven takes a swing at him, and he ducks. "Pressing your buttons, am I?" the man asks.

"Get the hell out of my home."

"What'd those kids ever do to you?" the man asks. "You lured them here, and then what'd you do with them?"

Steven grabs a handful of the man's shirt, pulling him forward, and is about to clock him when something black and sinuous falls out of the man's inside coat pocket. It's a wire.

"You're wiretapped," says Steven in a marveling voice. "You're not a book appraiser. You're a police plant."

Although I have no idea what the black cord means and haven't heard the term *wiretapped* before, I do know the word *police*. Steven's in deep trouble.

They think he's responsible for those teens, to the degree that they sent a fake book appraiser into the house. I immediately intention back to Miles and Phoebe. They need to know.

I find Miles and Phoebe talking with Dee. They both turn around when I appear, looking aggravated. It seems I interrupted something; maybe they were making progress with her, getting her to talk about what happened in the woods.

"Things are getting worse by the moment," I blurt, by

way of explanation. "Phoebe, a policeman is in the library talking to Steven. He pretended to be interested in the book collection."

"See?" says Phoebe to Dee, with more than a tinge of anger in her voice. "They think my dad killed you. You have to help us. I know it's awful to think about it, but you've got to help us. An innocent man is being blamed."

"Dee," says Miles in a softer voice. "We want to help you. You'll feel so much better when you can get out of here. You know what I mean?"

"I never should have come here," says Dee, and her voice cracks on the last word.

I look at Phoebe. It seems as if it's all she can do not to shake Dee. I've observed over our short acquaintance that she is not a very patient person.

"Just start from the beginning," says Miles. "You were at home, and you heard about the swords, so you wanted to come."

Dee nods, rubbing the outer corner of her eyes. She's not crying yet; it's like a preemptive gesture. "Everyone's always curious about the manor house," she says. "And when I heard they found swords, it just sounded so exciting. Like the Indiana Jones movies."

"So you set out on foot."

"I rode my bike, actually, and then ditched it. There were too many roots in the path once I got into the woods. I propped it up against a tree and just kept going."

"Okay, good. So you walked for a while," says Phoebe. "Then what?"

"I . . . I . . ."

"You . . . ?" says Phoebe.

I reach over and tug at her shirt. She doesn't need to be

sarcastic to this poor girl. "My father's going to be arrested. Can you help us out?"

"I'm trying. So . . . I just felt this force or something that was luring me, that wanted me to come a certain way. I left the path and walked through the trees. It seemed like it was getting darker, and suddenly I got worried about whether I would get lost."

"You had your phone with you?" says Miles.

"I did but I forgot to charge it. I knew I was on the last bit of the battery. So then I thought, I better go back and find my bike and get out of here. And that's when . . . I don't know. It got dark."

I sneak a look at Miles. *Dark?*

"It felt like there were dozens of hands all over me, scratching. Pulling me every which way, like they were fighting over me."

"Who were they?" I ask.

"I couldn't see, it was all happening so fast, and like I said the forest got really dark. Like a cloud had covered the sun. And they were moving me around . . . so . . . so hard. I was upside down sometimes, rolling around in their hands like in the surf when a wave knocks you over."

Phoebe steps forward and hugs her. Miles puts a hand on her shoulder. I do nothing, still held back by my centuries of training.

"I'm so sorry," says Phoebe.

"It was terrifying, and I knew it was the end," says Dee. "And then my skin was frigid cold and I saw weird, glowing . . . I don't know how to describe them. Signs or symbols or something."

"Can you describe them better?" asks Miles.

"Almost like . . . ancient letters or something."

"Runes!" says Phoebe instantly, with a hint of exult in her voice. "The tree! The tree under the pond."

"Time to pay a visit," says Miles.

"I'm not going," says Dee. "No way."

"But . . ." says Miles helplessly. It's difficult for him to say, *We'll find your body there and you'll be released to whatever Heaven or Hell awaits you.*

"We'll go," says Phoebe firmly. "You stay here. Don't move."

She throws me a look and I know she means to say that after we figure out what's going on with the tree, we'll provide a firm-armed escort there for Dee.

"I won't," says Dee. Her eyes are wide, and I feel sympathy for her state. She made a mistake and paid for it with her life.

We intention to the pond. There's the long wooden dock with a hole toward the end of it. It brings back a flood of feelings. I was so terrified that day . . . and when it was over, I thought everything was over. Yet, we still haunt the manor, in some ways as feeble as Dee.

Last time we were here, we let Phoebe do the hard work. Miles and I had stayed above water, anxious. This time I wasn't going to let that happen. If we were all three equal, we needed to share the danger equally.

"Are we ready?" I ask.

Miles slips his hand into mine, and I watch him do the same with Phoebe. "No one let go," he says.

We go to the edge of the pond and walk in. It's such a strange sensation to know I *should* be feeling wet. I look over at Phoebe. She's experiencing the pond differently from me and Miles. Her pants do show the water line increasing as we walk farther in. I remember that she had been soaking wet last time, but then had instantly dried off.

"Is it cold for you, Phoebe?" I ask.

"A bit," she says.

We walk until the water level is at my face and then we are under. Instantly I see the shattering glow that makes me close my eyes.

"My God," says Miles. Through the tug on my hand, I feel him stop.

"Just close your eyes," I say.

We continue forward. I feel the light so strongly on my face, a sort of diluted heat. We must be very close to the tree now.

We halt.

"You two are going to have to look," says Phoebe.

"All right," says Miles.

I mentally count to three and open my eyes. It's ghastly, horrifying, a stark upended network of black against the amber glow . . . and threaded through the twigs and drowned branches are three bodies.

They're extended as if the tree had taken pleasure in stretching them. Almost as if they had been caught in a spider's web: one hand here, an arm folded behind here, legs splayed or in the motion of running, hair fanned out, fingers spread, mouths open, eyes open, everything open.

It's Dee and Alexander and the third shape, black and witchy, thankfully her face turned from ours.

Still the glaring blaze from the tree, its runes seemingly on fire, broadcasting through the dark water to create an amber glow. They ripple as if with energy. They hurt my eyes.

What could they mean, these strange shapes etched on the

tree and alive with fire? They are the symbols some ancient peoples used to communicate. They are throbbing, fiercely aching to tell their tale here, but the glow is buried underwater. Only we see it.

"Well, mission accomplished," says Miles. "Let's go back up."

"We have to try to release their bodies," says Phoebe. "How else are they going to be found? No one's going to dive into the pond."

I look uneasily at Phoebe. I'm scared to go closer to that tree—perhaps it will ensnare me as well.

"But we have no corporeality," says Miles. "How can we release them?"

"Sometimes I can touch things," says Phoebe. "I have to try. Dee and Alexander will haunt us until their bodies are discovered."

"Don't get too close to her," says Miles, indicating the darker shape with a lifting of his chin.

Phoebe walks to Dee, impossibly entangled, and tries to free her hand from the tree. Dee's hair wafts in the small current, her eyes open and vacant. Phoebe can't help her. Her hands go right through Dee's body.

She tries at her waist, her other arm, her head, all to no avail. She works on Alexander's body next. I see the scratches that deepen his cheeks. Was it people who scratched him . . . or the tree? What on earth happened to him and Dee?

"Frustrating," says Phoebe. "All right, let's go back up."

Back on the banks of the pond, we look at one another. "We'll have to somehow tell your parents," I say.

But Phoebe shakes her head. "That would make it worse for Steven, if he knows where the bodies are. The police would ask him why he knows, how he knows."

She's right. It's a horrible situation. We want the bodies to be found so Dee and Alexander can be released, so they can "graduate" on to whatever the next realm of existence is for them . . . but we don't want Steven blamed for their deaths.

"Did the tree kill them?" Miles asks.

We stare at the dark oval of the pond. Were the teens attacked and then thrown into the water? Who did that to them, so young and innocent and harmless?

"We have to keep a really close eye on Tabby," says Phoebe. "Whatever happened to these guys, it *cannot* happen to her."

CHAPTER NINE

It's something I'm dying to know, what a sword blow feels like. Like, instant, incapacitating pain? Because it's not just sharp but it's got all this momentum coming off it since it's freaking long and someone's whole arm is engaged in swinging it down. I'm not recommending anyone go out and, uh, find out empirically LOL. I'm just talking. You lot keep your skin on your bones, okay?

—Online forum Knights in Dirty Armor

We intention back to the manor, where Tabby is again building a tower out of blocks. They are crookedly persisting. Steven is reading through a thick, ancient book, while Phoebe's mother is getting dinner ready.

Phoebe sinks down next to her sister with a sigh. "This is getting pretty old," she says, "watching over my sister as if she's going to get attacked at any minute."

I study my friend's beauty. I haven't known her long, but her face now feels more familiar than my own, unglimpsed in a mirror these many centuries. I find her lovely and unsettling. Her auburn hair had floated around her face when we were underwater, as if she floated in a bathtub, her eyes keen, her mouth always about to saying something she'd regret. She has power over Miles . . . but more so over me.

I hate her impetuous impulses, her taking Miles as her own before I even knew what was happening. I'll own that there is much good to her—her fierceness around her sister, her intelligence—but lodged in her beautiful half-open lips are enchanting words that will spell my destruction. How I love her . . . and how I despise her with every aching part of my mind and body.

"If I could drink the Sangreçu blood," I say, musing aloud, "I could save your father from suspicion. With corporeality, I could confess to the murders, bring the police to Dee and Alexander's bodies."

She looks at me, and I see no expected gratefulness. Instead she is wary, loath even to nod to this idea. She is the reason there is no more Sangreçu blood for me to drink.

"They would imprison me and the parents would get their chance to spit at me in my jail cell," I continue. "And then when the effect wore off, as it did for you and Miles, I'd be myself again"—how I cringe to think I have just characterized my dead and powerless state as "myself"—". . . and I would slip away."

She smiles briefly. A pang to my heart, if I can admit to it now. Even as I know she is perilous to my fate, I want to run my fingers down the side of her face.

"I would be the murderess who somehow escaped from her holding cell and confounded all their expectations," I say.

"I'd love to be a fly on the wall when they review the surveillance tape from your cell and see that you simply disappear," says Miles.

Phoebe nods. "We could be," she says. "The dead *are* the flies on the wall."

"It's a brilliant idea, Eleanor," says Miles. "Except we have no idea where the vials are."

I look at Phoebe, and she has the grace to look down.

"There must be some here at the manor," I say. "Madame Arnaud cleared out the cache when she left France, and brought them with her."

"There isn't an inch of this manor house we haven't explored," says Miles.

"Then we have to think about where they could be hidden."

"Go for it," says Phoebe flatly.

Miles casts a sympathetic look at me. It's all we've been thinking about for the last number of months, where the cache could be. Just wanting a thing doesn't bring it to your hands, alas.

"I'll be back later," I mutter, casting a glance at Tabby's tower in the second before it crashes to the ground. I hear her wail, cut off as if by treason, as I intention to the older part of the manor.

I'm in the main entry, on the grand, sweeping staircase. Light is muddled here, plodding in through thick, mullioned windows. I'm staring up at the stained glass window on the landing, the two knights battling each other. It's a clue somehow. Perhaps the weapons the men wield are the very same ones the bulldozer dug up.

I look at the anger and bewilderment in the men's faces. I can tell by the uplifted sword in one's hand, and the frighteningly positioned spear in the other's, that something cataclysmic is about to happen. This is the instant before the blades hit flesh. Which man conquered? Which one fell in a pool of his own blood? It's impossible to tell. The glassmaker didn't choose to show destiny on their faces, with one a clear victor.

I look again at the *XXX* marking. What does it mean?

Then . . . it hits me for the first time. There is a slight space between the first and second letter.

It's not *XXX*.

It's *X XX*.
Not thirty, but ten twenty.
Or . . . perhaps . . . I clap my hand to my mouth . . .
. . . perhaps the tenth month and the twentieth day.
October 20.

Back with Miles and Phoebe, I tell them what I've learned.
"Yes!" says Phoebe, exulting. "This battle must've taken place on October 20, and we were all born on that day. It's significant."

"No epic battles spring to mind as having taken place in October," says Miles.

"Uh . . . do you know the dates of *any* battles?" asks Phoebe.

Miles gives her a glare mixed with a smile. "D-day, June 6. Pearl Harbor, December 7. Bastille Day, July 14 . . ."

"Okay, you made your point."

"Effectively, I might add," he says.

"Well, it's helpful to have something to search for," says Phoebe. "Let's hit the manor library, and I'll see if there's anything about October battles."

We intention there and Miles and I walk the shelves looking for books about medieval warfare. Miles works his way to one of the dark alcoves, his head cocked to the side to read the titles on the spines. Is there anything so pleasing to the eye as a handsome young man selecting a book?

"I'm finding nothing," Phoebe calls out to us. I'm on top of one of the ladders to reach the top level of books, too high for a human to even stand on tiptoe and see, although that is a trick of the mind to make myself more comfortable. I could easily just hover here in midair.

"Hardly surprising," I say calmly. "We don't expect to

find it within mere minutes when the truth has been hidden for so many years."

"I should've shaken an explanation out of that damn Raven Gellerman when I had the chance," mutters Miles, thinking we can't hear him at this distance. I remain silent. Instead of trying to find out information about the secret society, he had been trying to reach out to his parents. And that time, unfortunately, he had been ineffective.

I look down from above as Phoebe next turns her attention to the book the appraiser was holding when the truth came out that he was working with the police. She idly turns pages, and then I hear a sharp intake of her breath.

"I found it! Oh my God, I found it!" she cries out.

Miles runs to her as I scramble down the ladder as fast as I can.

"Look at this!" she says, pointing to a paragraph. "The Battle of Camlann. The ancient Celts had a thirteen-month year, but this historian tracked the battle down to what we would call October 20."

I lean over to look. There's a small woodcut illustration at the top of the page, and it's very similar to the stained glass scene. Phoebe reads the passage aloud. "'At Camlann, Arthur was killed by his own son Mordred, and in turn killed him. Their weapons reached their goals of the moment, and both hearts, one true, one foul, bled out their essence. A brutal instance where king and heir died on the same inhale.'"

I raise my eyes to Miles, but his are fastened on Phoebe's face.

"The King Arthur legend," I murmur.

"Oh my God," she breathes. "Miles is Arthur. He's *Arthur*! Can you even doubt it?" She whirls around to me. "Look at his face. He's been noble all along, and now it's clicking into place!"

Miles sinks to his knees, and I see pain cross his face. "Oh my God," he says.

"Are you quite all right?" I ask. I crouch next to him and look anxiously into his eyes.

"I can see the sword flashing again," he says. "Like I did right after we drank from the vials." He puts both hands to his forehead as if he's been struck by a terrible headache.

"Stay calm," I say. "It's all in the past."

"But it isn't, is it?" he says with a surprising bit of anger.

"Our graduation has to do with righting the wrongs on the field of Camlann?" Phoebe asks.

"The devil if I know," he says. "All I know is that I killed someone, and then the grass was full of my own blood." His voice trails off in a wrenching wail.

I smooth his hair back. I want to press a kiss to that pained forehead. How awful to have slain his son for treachery and to be dealt a death blow instantaneously.

He sinks even farther, pressing closer to the ground, as if he can reclaim all that spilled blood somehow.

"You are not that same person," I say. "You have your own soul."

"But his soul is intermingled with mine," says Miles, looking up at both of us with a tortured expression. "You felt it, too, Phoebe, don't deny it."

She nods.

"I hurt someone, too," she says.

"*Killed*," says Miles with emphasis.

She looks hurt, but then nods. "I must have," she whispers.

"My family has long boasted of a connection to kings long dead," says Miles. "Is it possible I'm some sort of reincarnation of Arthur? It's head-spinning."

"Our whole world has been head-spinning recently," says Phoebe.

They both look at me, and the thoughts on their faces are transparent. Who am *I*? What might I have seen had I drunk from the vial with them?

"I have my own soul," says Miles. "I'm not reincarnated, but a different *kind* of reincarnated, perhaps, with snatches of a prior soul merged with mine, do you think?"

"Perhaps the Sangreçu blood didn't just make you aware of a former life, but imparted it," I suggest.

Phoebe snorts. "As if there were lives embedded in the blood?"

"No," says Miles firmly. "It was like the blood simply opened the curtain and showed me what had been there already."

"So then, if you have vestiges of Arthur's soul in you, then who am I?" Phoebe asks. "Guinevere?"

A rush of emotion fills my head. "That would explain your feelings for Miles," I say stiffly. "But there is no way, no possible way, that you were a woman of such nobility and good breeding."

"Thanks a lot," she says sarcastically.

"I will say that you were a very bewitching lady nonetheless," I add. And then red-hot rage fills me. I stare at her beautiful face with such hatred I know it must be visible on mine. What on earth did Phoebe—or some version of Phoebe—*do* to me?

Miles seems unaware, however, of my anger. "So does that make you Launcelot, Eleanor?" He laughs as he says it.

He stops when he realizes no one else is laughing.

I take one last tortured look at Phoebe, and intention myself away. I can't be with her right now; it's too painful.

I return several hours later. They're poring over the book, continuing to read about Arthur. They tell me that although Arthur died on the battlefield, when his sword Excalibur was thrown back into the lake, three fairy queens came to take his body away to the island of Avalon. There it was reputed they had healed him, and he slept in a hollow hill awaiting the day he could return.

"Arthur isn't dead," says Phoebe. "He's part of you."

"Somewhere he's lying, perhaps seeing flashes of me as I see flashes of him?" asks Miles quietly.

No one responds. We have no answers, only guesses.

CHAPTER TEN

The hieroglyphics tell so many strange tales that are incomprehensible to us now, remnants of a vanished culture. In the since-crumbled lesser temple at Bubastis, a horned creature is depicted feasting on the neck of a man held down on his pallet by two others. In the next scene, the man arises, green as Osiris, with punctures dripping blood that is caught by a bowl held by a priestress. This has in part given rise to ideas of blood drinking and vampirism in the ancient Egyptian world.

—*Vampyres: Bram, Bathory, and Beyond*

*T*he next morning, the book on the kitchen table is open to an entry about Egyptian vampires.

"He's so off base," says Phoebe, frowning.

"Well, let's focus on our own prophecy, then," I say. "Didn't the first line say something about a king? It could be King Arthur."

"'On a stronde the king doth slumber, and below the mede the dragon bataille,'" Miles recites from memory.

"A stronde," I repeat. "Perhaps that is an archaic rendering of the word *strand*?" They both look at me blankly. "Perhaps *strand* is itself an archaic word to you. It means *beach*."

"On a beach the king does slumber," says Phoebe.

Yes. It is like the moment that kindling catches fire. Phoebe and Miles had sequestered themselves on a beach once. It must be meaningful.

"And below the something, the dragon . . . er . . . does something."

"*Bataille* looks like *battle*," comments Phoebe.

"*Mede* could be an elder form of *meadow*," I say. And of course the meadow means something to me.

We're meant to restore King Arthur to the throne, I think with a catch in my throat. What a responsibility, and what a thoroughly mind-altering task. For me, Arthur was simply the man of legend, and if I had thought about him when I was a girl, I imagined he might be someone that time and adoration had built up into something more illustrious than what he truly was. He had done well in battle, so well that they believed his sword to be magic, and invented a tale around its coming to him from the wet hand of the Lady of the Lake. They had invested him with a magical coun-selor, a wizard named Merlin. All these fanciful tales had embroidered the truth of a man who lived a short and brutal life. But what if the legends were true, and Arthur was as remarkable as told?

"What is the next line?" asks Phoebe.

After some rummaging, she locates the secret societies book under a pile of similar tomes in Steven's den.

"'. . . the dragon bataille the wicked brike with bisemare from yon damosel,'" reads Miles.

Deplorable. How ever can we decipher this? What on earth is a brike? And what is a bisemare?

"*Damosel* may be *damsel*," says Phoebe.

"So the damsel has or gives the wicked brike some bise-mare?"

"I wish my effin' phone would work!" Phoebe shouts. "This is so frustrating! It would take me five seconds to Google *bisemare*!"

Miles looks at my face and explains what she means. Googling allows a person to access all the information the world has, instantly. I shake my head. It's too much to under-stand. It seems like magic on a level with Madame Arnaud's.

I have to, for now, set aside my disbelief. "But with this

wondrous invention, why doesn't Raven Gellerman decode the prophecy?" I ask. "Certainly the older members of the group may not understand or know of this resource, but she would, don't you think?"

Miles looks at me surveyingly. "Absolutely, she would," he says slowly. "So why is she behaving like there's no way to figure it out?"

Perhaps there is more to Raven than we knew. She is deliberately obscuring the meaning of the prophecy. Does she stand to gain in some way?

"Was *she* born on October 20?" Phoebe asks.

"We need to find out more about her," says Miles. "Let's see where she is now. I'll take you."

Raven's with Steven.

I can't believe it.

They're standing close as lovers on the crest of a stone bridge over one of the streams on the estate. I remember when the bridge was first built, a thin affair to hold only two people abreast. We servants had taken great joy in crossing it on our free day.

"That's Raven?" Phoebe asks, her voice tight. "What's Steven doing with her?"

"It isn't every man that can do what you can," Raven tells Steven, with flattery and admiration in her voice.

"It's all for you," he says. I can't believe his voice, suddenly thickly English. Steven has always struck me as someone who lived in the States long enough that his accent eroded. Today it is back and thick as if he'd lived in Grenshire all his life.

Phoebe puts her hand to her mouth in horror.

"In another year you can divorce her," says Raven.

He nods, and Phoebe lets out a sob that brings Miles instantly to her side, pulling her into his arms.

"But why wait?" says Steven, still with that uncanny accent.

"Give her another year of thinking you're hers. I'll be eighteen in a year," says Raven. "I'll take her place, and I'll make you much, much happier." She leans backward against the bridge, both hands bracing her weight on the stone wall. She looks like she is arranging herself for a kiss.

"I'll do whatever you wish," says Steven.

Phoebe vanishes, and a second later Miles does, too, gone to comfort her. I stay and watch. Why is Raven making such forward advances to a man so much older, who is married and with a young child to boot?

"Do you think you can do what we've asked?" says Raven.

"Of course," says Steven.

"You say that each time but do something slightly different."

He hangs his head. "I try."

"Give me a chaste kiss and do my bidding."

"Yes, my lady," he says.

She bites down on her lip and whimpers as blood appears. I draw closer, confused and fascinated. Steven's eyes lower as if he is about to swoon, and he presses closer to her. "Give me a chaste kiss," she repeats. He presses his lips to her for a mere second and he does as she wishes, a brief kiss with little emotion in it. As he withdraws, I see her blood on his lower lip.

"It scares me," he says. "I don't want to do it."

"But you must."

"Now?" he asks.

"It is the perfect time."

"I'll go," he says.

She makes a funny motion with her hands, almost as a spell would look. She turns one direction on the bridge, and he another. They part without saying another word.

I stand stunned, in disbelief about what I've just seen. Raven asked Steven to kill—there's no other interpretation, is there? I frantically try to review their conversation to see if it can be construed any other way.

Raven's face as she passes me is bland and satisfied. She walks at the kind of pace you'd use to fetch a broom when you're not in a hurry.

But Steven . . . he's alternately hurrying and then slowing almost to a standstill. I catch up to him.

"Steven," I urge. "Don't do this."

He doesn't see me, doesn't hear me. His eyes are wide and his hands tremble. I try to take his hand, without success.

"Steven!" I scream into his ear, and he doesn't even blink.

I whirl in a frustrated circle. I can't stop him. I'll have to tell Phoebe, and she can use Tabby to get through to him or her mother. But in the meantime . . . he's going to murder someone.

If I could just find the Sangreçu vials, I could fix everything: stop Steven, bring the bodies to the surface, tell Raven's parents their daughter is involved in something awful. I could use one of those mobiles and figure out the wording of the prophecy—and enact it. I could earn my forever peace and see if Austin is on the other side waiting for me.

Blood is everything. It opens all the doors, makes a man do a girl's bidding.

Miles told me once that the vial he drank from had sung to him, hummed an allure like the mermaids bringing sailors to dash their ships against the rocks. Why can't I hear that tune? I know it is being sung somewhere on this estate. We haven't tried hard enough to find it. But that is because Miles and Phoebe are already Sangreçu. They don't care. They have supped at the table, and what do they care that I came in from the cold after the table was cleared?

I stand for a long time regarding the tree branch at the edge of the meadow, keeping Steven in my peripheral vision. No one passing by here today would ever know I swung from that branch, heavily swaying after my feet stopped kicking. It is unremarkable now, this scene of my former high pitch of distress.

And so the world passes. One person's end of the world is simply another day of buttering bread for another. My life didn't matter. Phoebe's didn't. Somehow Miles's did, though, because the world wouldn't let King Arthur die. We are his subjects and we must resurrect him.

I turn from the tree with disgust, regard instead the long pass of the meadow where wildflowers wag their thoughtless heads. I must be pragmatic, must solve this problem like the dairymaid keeping the bucket from being kicked over. I will calm the cow, soothe its stress. I will find the vial or vials. Methodically.

Wherever they are.

I formulate a plan. I need to see the blueprints for the manor. Madame Arnaud had it built when she escaped from France.

The plans for the grounds.

The outbuildings, stables, chapel, all of it.

There must be a clue. A walled-off chamber, a secret passageway: something will show me the place Madame Arnaud built to house the vials she stole.

Phoebe may be able to touch the blueprints since they would be original to the home, but she doesn't know where they are. Only Steven knows. I check his progress and see to my relief that he's clearly heading back to the manor. Did he change his mind, resist Raven's dictate, or was he always on his way there?

The tree is now a stark outline against the blue twilight. Time to go back.

When I find Phoebe, she's cursing the influence of Raven. "It's not Steven's fault," she's telling Miles. "Raven has put some kind of spell on him. He loves my mom."

Miles says nothing. I wonder, should I tell them it looks like Steven really is responsible for Dee's and Alexander's deaths? I worry that if I do, she won't be able to recover enough to be helpful. She's already upset thinking he's guilty only of intended adultery. Maybe I'll tell Miles later, when we have some time alone. But for now, my focus is narrow: we have to find those vials.

"That evil little bitch," says Phoebe. "My mom's had enough to deal with. Having her husband cheat on her with jailbait is just . . ."

"You're right," I say when her voice trails off. "Steven's innocent and this is all Raven's doing. She's trying to manipulate things so she benefits from the prophecy."

Miles puts his head in his hands. I'm lying and he knows it. Anytime a grown man is involved with a girl, it's wrong and his fault. He's the adult.

"So we have to figure out the prophecy before her and get

Steven out of her grasp," I continue. "And the key to that is the vials."

"You think so?"

"It's the only way. So we have to look at the manor blueprints. Get Tabby to tell Steven to pull them out for us. Then we can rescue him from Raven."

"Thank you," she says. She gives me a weak smile, and I'm pleased that she was so easy to convince.

"No time to waste," I say.

We have decided, the three of us, that the word to focus upon is *blueprints*. So this is the word Phoebe is firmly and insistently supplying to Tabby's ear. Tabby reacts as if a housefly keeps buzzing near her earlobe.

"It's me, Tabby," she says finally in exasperation. "I'm always here. You know that. So hear me!"

But Tabitha instead asks her mother for permission to watch television, which is granted, and then Phoebe must struggle over the loud voices of actors on this incredible contraption.

"Anyone else want to try?" asks Phoebe glumly, looking from Miles to me.

"She never knew me," I say.

"Why not?" says Miles. "It's worth a shot." He kneels next to Tabby and begins the monotonous repetition. I watch her face carefully. She's hearing something, all right, since she keeps twitching away from that affected ear. But she seems bent on ignoring it.

Is it possible Tabby is knowingly cutting off contact with her dead sister?

Perhaps it is too painful for her, little dear girl.

"Break it up into two words," I suggest. "*Blue* and *prints*. Any child knows the color blue."

"Blue," says Miles firmly.

Tabby sighs, a deep, strangely adult sound. "Boo," she repeats.

Phoebe jumps up, elated. "You did it, Miles! You got to her!"

"Prints," Miles says.

There's a very long pause. "Pince," says Tabby.

"That's right, sweetie! Blue. Prints."

"Boo. Pince."

"Okay, great. Go tell Steven."

Obediently, Tabby gets up and goes over to her father. "Boo. Pince," she says carefully as she crawls up into his lap.

I watch Phoebe's face. She's clearly struggling not to be enraged at Steven. Placing all the blame at Raven's door is helping, but not completely.

Steven buries his face into her hair in a long, sweet hug. "Hello, adorable," he says. "What was that you said?"

"Boo."

"Ooh, don't scare me!" he says.

"*Boo*," she says.

"But I don't want to be scared!" he says, thinking he's playing along.

"Boo . . . boo pants," she says.

"Prints!" shouts Phoebe. She gets control of herself and goes over to say the word in Tabby's ear.

"Pince," amends Tabby.

Steven's laughing at her cuteness, and I see Tabby's frustration increasing. She's already doing something she doesn't want to do, and now he can't seem to hear her message.

"Blueprints," repeats Phoebe, and her little sister does her best. "Boo pince."

"Ooh, a blue prince?" says Phoebe's mum. "That's a neat thing to think about. His crown has sapphires in it?"

Phoebe gives her mum the kind of look I believe would not have been abided by my own mother. Disbelief mixed with scorn. It is not a pleasant look, and not one her mother deserves.

"Seriously? She's going with *blue prince* instead of *blueprints*?" says Phoebe.

"It is so hard when two things sound like each other," I murmur.

"Boo pince!" screams Tabby at the top of her lungs.

That gets everyone's attention. Can Tabby hear us? Is she constantly distracted by the two conversations going on, one "real" and understood and heard by the living, and the other interrupting, confusing, distracting?

"She's giving us a message," says Phoebe's mother. "It's something from Phoebe." She kneels at Steven's feet and looks intensely in Tabby's face. "What does that mean, sweetie? Can your sister tell us more?"

"Floor plans," says Phoebe promptly.

"Foor pans," says Tabby.

"Four pans . . . ?" Phoebe's mum looks at Steven with a huge frown. "I want to understand . . ."

Tabby bursts into tears. "Oh, sweetie, it's all right, it's all right," says Phoebe's mum. "It's fine."

"I understand," says Steven. "She's saying *blueprints* and *floor plans*. Phoebe must want to see them for the manor. She's onto something."

"Yes!" Phoebe exults. She looks at Miles wildly, and he flashes her the kind of smile that makes my heart leap. If only it were aimed at me.

"It's fine, Tabby, please don't cry," pleads her mum, her own eyes full of tears. "I love you, Phoebe," she says to the air.

"I'll get them now," says Steven. "I'll spread them over the table. If you can take her, Anne?"

"Of course." Phoebe's mum pulls Tabby off his lap into a long hug. He stands and looks around the room.

"Are you here, Phoebe?" he asks. "I love you."

A long pause ensues. I'm waiting for her to say it back, even if he can't hear it, but she just can't do it.

CHAPTER ELEVEN

While I was at my bath last Saturday, my keys were taken, for I heard them jingling. I rose and shouted and heard the clink of them falling back onto the table, and although I hastened out as quickly as I could, the culprit had long since fled. This is not a crime of mere mischief, but a dreadful and dire one that will lead to the immediate punishment and sacking of the offender. If you've heard talk of such a prank, come to me with your intelligence, for I do not consider it a light transgression.

—Miss Sneldam's address to the gathered staff

*T*he plans, carefully spread by Steven onto the dining room table, are written in a spidery hand, archaic even to my eye. I stare at the outlines of rooms I once worked in, bedchambers where I hauled coal and scraped ashes and cinders into a dustbin. I see rendered as parallel lines the staircases where I scurried up and down to do Madame Arnaud's bidding.

The blueprints show towers at the top of the house. I had never been in them, only seen them from the ground, glass and iron that seemed to reflect the sun in a blinding way.

We look at the cellars, where musty-smelling rooms housed hundreds of wine bottles, where we stored vegetables and twine-wrapped meats. Phoebe trails a finger over the passageways that, in true life, haven't been walked in lifetimes.

"What is this?" asks Miles. He points to where we can see the faint edge of another piece of paper laid atop the map. The ink on this paper is a slightly different color, perhaps added much later so time aged it differently, or perhaps inked with a different batch. The paper shows three chambers, marked as *storage*.

"What do you think is under there?" I ask. "Is it significant, or simply an area where an error was made?"

"One way to find out," says Phoebe.

We intention to the dark cellars. It is black as pitch and I can't see a thing. I hear Miles utter a foul word.

"We need light," says Phoebe glumly. "Time to go talk to Tabby again."

"Wait," I say. "In the parts of the cellars I had been into before, there were flares set in the walls and here and there the maids left boxes of lucifers tucked in between the stones. If no one has moved them, they should still be here."

"Lucifers?" she asks, her voice suddenly close. She has moved toward me in the dark.

"I think she means matches," says Miles.

I wait. It's so dark I nearly intention away, but I force myself to stay calm and remain. Nothing can hurt me now, but I still feel the tremulous waves of fear rush over me.

"I think I have it," says Phoebe. She rustles around and then suddenly I hear the *zzzppshh* of a lucifer coming to light. A glow now surrounds her face, floating in the black like a lotus sitting on dark water. She looks around, spies a flare and lights it. Now we can see our surroundings, the arched stone passageway of the cellar.

"This is where the three storage rooms are," says Miles. "Let's see what's stored inside."

Phoebe tries each door but they are locked.

"Any idea where the maids hid the keys?" she asks me.

"You might try the lintel?"

She does but there are no hidden keys.

"Another dead end," Miles observes.

"Do not lose hope so quickly now," I advise. "There must be a way inside."

Of course we could intention—but then we wouldn't have the flare to see with.

"Didn't someone have a large ring of keys?" Miles asks. "Jangling around like you see on *Downton Abbey*?"

"The head housekeeper did," I agree. "But when the house was abandoned, whatever did she do with them?"

"Probably threw them down a well," says Phoebe. "Or the . . . whatever you call a bathroom."

"The privy," I say, and for a second I indulge in a soft laugh, thinking of stiff-mannered Miss Sneldam detaching her ring and letting it go down into the malodorous pit. She'd always been so firm with her underlings, and yet we knew she harbored affection for us despite our shortcomings.

"Phoebe, can you kick the door down?" asks Miles. "It's probably half rotted with all the damp down here anyway."

And thus ensues a period of time in which Miles winks endlessly at me and tries to not let Phoebe see his bouts of laughter that bend him double as she kicks the door and throws her shoulder against it like a demon in a fit. I find I must succumb to merriment, too, and I am far less proficient at hiding it than he. Phoebe whirls around and catches us.

"Glad I'm amusing you while I'm working my butt off trying to break down the door."

"It looks like things are more solid down here than we might've thought," says Miles.

"Can I just say how much it sucks being the only person on this team who can touch things?" she demands.

"You can say it, but we don't believe it for a second," says Miles. "You were clearly a successful door kicker in life."

"Why do I get the feeling *door kicker* is some weird English insult?"

"It's so sad you can never seem to trust me," says Miles silkily, and at that the fun ends for me.

"Cannot you use a bent nail?" I ask impatiently.

"Throw one at me and I'll try it," she says.

"I'm sure she would, happily, if she could," says Miles.

"Look in the dust along the floor," I say. "Surely something must have dropped down there that we can use. No one ever wielded a broom on these shadows, I'm sure."

I crouch and look, hoping for some dull glint of something we can use.

"Keys don't simply fall to the ground because you want them to," says Phoebe.

"Oh no?" I counter. I point. "This looks to be exactly that."

"Are you effin' kidding me?" Miles asks.

He peers into the gloom until Phoebe's hand plucks the dusty bit of bronze and wipes it off. "It's a key, all right," she says.

It doesn't work on the first door or the middle door. Just as I am grinding my teeth with frustration, the key moves within the lock of the third door. "It's turning!" says Phoebe.

Of course, the door sticks and again Phoebe applies vengeance to its wooden affront, but this time it works and the door reluctantly opens with a groan and a scrape against the stone floor.

With Phoebe leading us, we enter.

The space is large. In fact, I turn to look at the door we have entered through, and note that all three doors lead to the same space. Just as the map intimated, the three storage rooms are not as they seem and are instead one cavernous room.

There are no furnishings, no windows, no adornment of any kind.

"Do you hear anything, Miles?" asks Phoebe. "Are the vials singing?"

"Maybe," he says. "I hear something faint."

He kneels at one of the flagstones in the middle of the room. "It's coming from here," he says.

There's nothing special about the stone; no one but Miles would ever notice it to be different from all the others. Phoebe puts the flare into a wall sconce and then crouches and touches the stone.

"Is it a trip to a secret door?" she wonders aloud.

"Give it all your weight," says Miles.

She presses as hard as she can, to no avail. Then she runs her fingers around the edges of the stone.

"Perhaps you are meant to lift it up?" I ask.

She tries.

"It's like a steering wheel," she observes. "I'll just . . . drive." She grasps the stone on either side with both hands and then twists. The stone begrudgingly moves with a scraping sound. It rotates until it is released, and she pushes it onto the stones next to it.

"Nice driving," comments Miles.

"Better than yours," she says.

There's a moment where Miles and I both inhale, taken aback at her audacity to refer so lightly to a horrible memory in his life.

Where the stone had been, there is darkness. Phoebe retrieves the flare and tries to light the vastness. "There's a staircase," she says.

She goes first with the light, and then me, and then Miles. The staircase is a narrow, grim, stone affair without banisters. It twists around so that I lose Phoebe's light each time she circles the main shaft of the stairs, a brute column. It's worse for Miles, so I reach back and take his hand to guide him.

We descend down, the air growing colder and mustier. I feel surrounded by frigid space; if I were yet breathing, I believe I'd see plumes of vapor emanating from my nose and mouth.

Finally, we reach the ground. Phoebe walks in a wide circle with the torch, but we can't see the limit of the walls. The chamber's vast.

"What is this place?" I ask. My voice sounds small and forlorn.

"I don't know, but I don't think it's storage," says Miles.

"Let's walk further," says Phoebe, and we follow her into the blackness, lit only by the pool of light that moves with us. In the distance, I hear water dripping, and then a louder sound as we grow closer. The walls glitter, and I see a grotto where a waterfall flows over moss-covered rocks. We are subterranean. The walls aren't walls; they're earth.

"This place is . . . it's not good," says Miles.

I realize we're still holding hands as his tightens. "Maybe we should return," he says.

"We have to know," says Phoebe.

I feel the unholiness radiating from the earthen walls. This place was where horrible things happened, and somehow far worse than what Madame Arnaud did seemingly miles above us in the manor. This is older, more settled in its malevolence.

As we continue forward, we come across a stone table of sorts, elevated above a dinner table's height.

We approach it.

"It hurts my ears," says Miles.

"What do you hear?" I ask.

"The lamenting," he says. "That thread of sound I've heard ever since I first came to the manor. It's emanating from here."

"From this room?"

"From this . . . thing."

"But it's not the Sangreçu vials?" I ask.

"I don't think so."

As we get closer, I see that the flat stone contains several holes and tubes that run from the table down into dug-out reservoirs in the floor. It looks like the tubes are meant to carry away blood, I think.

I look for bloodstains and see them. This table was not a place of innocence. People were slain here.

I believe this is an altar for ritual sacrifice.

"It's evil," says Miles, and as soon as the word passes his lips, I begin running back toward the staircase although it's now hidden to me in the gloom.

"Use intention!" Miles shouts behind me.

With a vast sense of relief, I remember that I don't have to run through darkness. I hurl myself mentally to a place I know like the back of my hand.

I'm in the meadow now, and it's past twilight, darkening quickly.

Miles is there with me, his breath ragged.

We look at each other with heartbreaking solemnity. Phoebe didn't come with us.

But there's no way we're going back there.

"This is a beautiful place," I say almost to myself. "I love the long grass rippling in the wind."

"It feels like a world away," says Miles.

This is what the earth offers, I think to myself. Humans do terrible things, but the grass keeps accepting the gentle persuasion of the breeze, and a tree lets its leaves flicker for the same. I will always find peace in nature's wholesome offerings.

"Hello! So glad to see some others in these godforsaken woods." I jolt at the too-loud voice right in my ear. "Do you know how to get back to the village?"

The middle-aged woman is modern, wearing a nubby beige sweater and loose-fitting jeans. "Did you see that creepy man? My name is Amey Adkins, by the way." I bite my lip. We haven't been watching Steven, and he must've snuck back out. I'm a fool . . . and it's *my* fault this woman is dead. I want to sink to my knees and howl.

"I'm Miles, and this is Eleanor. I don't think we saw him," Miles answers her after giving me a significant look.

"He gave me the creeps, out here all by himself."

"What did he look like?" Miles asks her.

"I don't know, a bit approaching six foot?"

"How old, and what color hair?" Miles doesn't seem to have noticed that I'm speechless.

"My age, I'd say," Amey answers. "Dark brown hair. He scared the wind out of me. I ran as fast as I could. I didn't think I went fast enough . . ." She trails off. "But I guess I did."

There is blood matted in her pale blond hair, and she, too, shows the scratches on her face. It's as if someone had been trying to write on her skin.

"Are those runes?" Miles asks me.

With shock, I realize he's right. The ancient symbols that glowed from the tree seem to be etched onto Amey's face.

"Are what ruins?" she asks.

I point across the meadow. "The ruins of an old house," I say. I can't bear the thought of her knowing her face is a missive from the force that killed her.

And it's all my fault.

"So many things to translate," says Miles. "Prophecies and runes." Amey luckily ignores this.

"Can you help me get home?" she asks. "I'm pretty well shook up, aren't I?"

"We'd love to help you," says Miles. "We would really love to."

"But you can't?" she asks plaintively.

"Not really, no."

She appeals to me, and I give her a sad smile. "You met with some trouble in the woods," I say kindly. "Desperately bad trouble. Did you know you were bleeding?"

Her hands go to her face and scalp and come back red. Her eyes widen. "I'm still bleeding!" she gasps. "I have to get to the hospital!" She frantically pats at her pockets. "I must've dropped my phone—can you ring an ambulance for me?"

"We know you're going through a tough patch," says Miles. "We've been through that same experience. What you're starting to realize."

"What I'm . . . what? Gosh, love, just call me a bloody ambulance, will you? I've been wandering these damn woods not knowing I was injured!"

"I can't call for you," he says. "I can't ever call again."

Amey stares at him. "Are you daft?"

"I can't do things the living can do," he says.

"The living . . . what on earth do you mean?"

"I'm not living anymore."

"So you're . . . ?"

"I'm dead," he confirms. "And so is Eleanor."

A significant passage of time elapses before she breaks into hysterical laughter. "Oh, you had me going there, I admit it, lad, you've yanked my chain and good!"

She quiets and I see the fear quivering behind her eyes. "These woods are so frightening," she whispers. "And now you two are scaring me, too. I need to go home."

"We won't hurt you," I say. "I'm sorry. I'm so sorry."

"The person who hurt you, we want to hear more about him," says Miles. "We want to stop him from hurting other people." I can't help myself from crying out. Miles doesn't know it's Steven. I was the only one with that crucial information and I failed to use it properly.

"He was just a man," she says. "I don't know any more than that. Well, if you won't help me, I'll just find my own way out. I hope I don't bleed to death on the way home. If I make it back, it's no thanks to you."

"All right," Miles says. "Good luck. But if you change your mind and want to see us again, just think of us and you'll find us."

"Not bloody likely," she mutters, and seems to randomly pick a course through the thicket. She seems unwitting of the idea that she makes no sound. No branches break underfoot, no leaves protest at her step.

"So the tree has human help," says Miles. "Do you think it's Phoebe's father?"

I wipe away a tear before he can see it. Servants must always keep an implacable demeanor.

"Yes," I say. "And I'll tell you why."

CHAPTER TWELVE

A maid's apron displays her pride of cleanliness and exactitude, for its wide, white expanse, however soiled from the day's work, emerges each morning gleaming bright again, its field free from wrinkles or smooches.

—*The Governance of Servants*

I didn't go to school past the age of eight. I know my letters and numbers all right—I kept a diary while alive although I can't pledge that every word is spelled correctly. I think my strength lies less in book learning and more in life learning. The servants bewailed their fate; I tried to change mine.

So I set my mind to untangling all the crooked skeins we'd been presented with. Austin and his family had talked of the pagan forces at the estate, and I now believe Madame Arnaud was aware of them, too. It seems she even built the house around an ancient sacrificial site. It's probably why she chose to come to Grenshire when she fled France. Her friend Athénaïs must've told her secrets, told her of the formidable forces here.

And . . . perhaps she, horrible as she was, somehow dampened the evil. She kept it in check while she was around, but since we removed her from her position of power, the evil has crept back in. It's our fault things have worsened. In trying to protect Tabby, we unleashed a far worse power. It somehow fastened onto Raven and then Steven.

So we must right the wrongs.

"I've never seen you frown harder," says Miles. "You're developing about three new wrinkles."

Back to this dismal world, where my cleverness isn't clever enough.

"I'm thinking," I say.

"And . . . ?"

"Blood was spilled at that table," I say. "It was an altar of sorts to some god we have thankfully forgotten."

"But has it forgotten us?"

I stare at him. "I hadn't really . . . thought about that."

"What *were* you thinking about?"

"The blood. The table seemed designed to capture the blood of a victim. What if vessels sat at the bottom of each tube to collect the blood? And what if that is the basis of the Sangreçu vials?"

"Impossible," says Miles. "Madame Arnaud built the manor after she left France."

"But don't you think the altar predates the manor? I believe she built the house around the subterranean vault, to protect it and keep it under her control and power."

He nods, a crooked smile beginning to form.

"So if the Sangreçu vials were created here, moved to France, and brought back, then perhaps they may be hidden in that same chamber."

"It seems as good a surmise as any," I say. "If Athénaïs created them here, she knew of this place and told Madame Arnaud."

"Good working hypothesis."

"So we'll need to explore better."

"The chamber that Phoebe is already exploring," he says. His eyes narrow. "She wasn't scared down there like we were."

"And she's the only one with the corporeality to actually explore," I point out. "We should hasten there at once."

"We should," he says, but somehow we still stand there, looking at each other. He takes a step closer, and before I can stop myself, I'm in his arms. His body is so strong, so large, unlike the reedy nature of my Austin, who never ate like this generation eats, who worked like a horse from sunup to sundown.

Miles's hands move into my hair and I greedily drink in his gaze.

"I so much admire you," he says, and my lips stop a mere inch away from his.

"Admire?" I ask.

"You've taught me everything I know."

I close my eyes. His feelings for me are not what I wish.

"I'm only what I am because of you," he continues.

"No," I whisper. "That was someone else."

"You're beautiful," he says.

"But not in the way you want," I say.

That seems to penetrate to him, and he frowns and shakes his head. But then he reverts to his strange, altered demeanor. "I always want your friendship, strong and true," he says. "And your guidance."

I step away. There will never be a kiss. He is not for me. The only lad who returned my feelings is long dead and cold in the grave. Austin was my one chance at love, and I ruined everything by tying my apron around my neck. If I'd only asked him to run away with me. Maybe we could've sailed to France, just as Athénaïs must have done all those centuries ago. Or gone north to Scotland, or west to Ireland. I had other choices but was desperate in my fear.

"Don't trust me to guide you," I say in a low voice. "I have steered my own course completely astray."

CHAPTER THIRTEEN

Oedipus's tyrannical ravings notwithstanding, we do find
him a sympathetic character, helpless before the grinding
mechanisms of fate. And what a fate it is: to murder his father
and know his own mother as a marital companion. Pressing
the horror further, he comes across her body, hanged in shame,
and pulls out her dress pins, revealing the nubile flesh for
which he has so destroyed himself, and uses the pins to blind
his eyes. And all of this while he was trying to *avoid* his cruel
prophecy! Poor king could only decipher one of the Sphinx's
riddles, it seems.

—*Mad Women (and Men) in Attic Tragedy*

*A*fter I explain everything, Miles announces that he'll be Steven's shadow until the end of time. "Not that I can stop him from anything," he says angrily, "but I'll sure as hell try."

As for me, I check in with Phoebe at the subterranean grotto. I don't like that place, and I shudder at the thought of returning, but if Phoebe's susceptible to evil the way Steven is, I have to try to intervene.

"Hullo," I say as I arrive.

Phoebe's sitting on top of the altar, her legs crossed. She's holding something in her hands. "Check this out," she says. "I can't stop looking at it."

It's a beautifully wrought silver rack. It's an object to behold even as my gut clenches with the sickening knowledge that it holds no vials. Empty and beautiful, it is left here to mock the seeker.

A glimmer of the past comes to me.

The man who created this. He's the same person who fashioned Madame Arnaud's silver straw, and the same armorer who hammered out our swords before they were magicked. Fading and brightening through the centuries as the same man in different iterations.

We are all just scraps of souls rebuilt from parts and sent out again to see how we fare. I can see his face if I concentrate, red from the smithy fire, whatever lifetime that fire burned in.

Where is he now? Is he yet in the world, bending silver to his will, or perhaps his trade has adapted and he sits at a computer instead of pulling beauty from molten metal. I can't know.

"You're taking this well," says Phoebe.

"There has to be more," I say. "It would be too cruel to keep us in this state if there wasn't a way to repair it."

"I don't know," she says.

"That's the point of prophecies," I say stubbornly. "No matter what, they work. Even when Oedipus is sent off as a child to be killed, the prophecy spares him so he can grow up to do the things he's slated to do."

"Okay, so there are just racks and racks of the stuff stashed everywhere, right?"

"Don't speak lightly of this, I warn you—"

"I know, I know, you'd be Sangreçu now if I hadn't been so greedy. I don't know how many times I can apologize for that."

I stare at her, and the old hatred rekindles.

"Perhaps . . . once would be fitting," I say.

"I have!"

"No, Phoebe, you never did."

"Oh my God, I must've."

I shake my head. She throws the rack, and it lands with a tinny crash. "Dammit, I'm sorry! I can't believe I didn't say it before, but I'm sorry. I wish I was a better person."

"The words are correct, but the tone is not," I say. "You're shouting at me."

"I'm shouting at myself, dammit! I screwed everything up. If I had just not died, I would've grown out of my selfishness."

I say nothing. Even her apology reeks of self-pity. She blames it all on having died.

"From the bottom of my heart, I'm sorry," she says quietly. "Is it better when I don't yell it?"

"Somewhat better."

She jumps down from the table and kicks the rack into the dark edges of the room.

"Can we leave now?" I ask. "This room has a very unpleasant demeanor."

In the morning, Miles is on Steven duty, and Phoebe and I follow her mother as she walks with Tabby outside the manor. The air is fresh and the grass sparkles with dew. They peer over the orange tape at the swords and then wander without purpose. Tabby walks with her hand in her mother's, such a sweet sight. There are no horses and carts to run them over—I adjust my thinking: no *cars* to run them over—so they don't need to be holding hands. And yet they do.

Tabby's mum says nursery rhymes and pauses to have her daughter supply words in the middle. She's visibly nervous, looking around quite a bit as if expecting someone to come hurtling toward them. I wager she is thinking of those missing teens.

Tabby, too, seems to be looking around, perhaps trying to sense her sister after the contact with her earlier when we got her to say *blueprints*.

". . . went up the hill to fetch a pail of . . . ?" asks Tabby's mum.

"Waddah," says Tabby.

"Very good!"

Phoebe smiles but I see pain in her face. All of this is happening without her. Tabby growing, changing, learning. Someday she'll surpass Phoebe in age, a teenager whom they maybe won't let swim.

I'm feeling too raw from our encounter in the grotto. I can't bear to feel pity for her, so I wave my hand gently and move away, aimless in the wind. I wonder if it might snow. There is a chill and bluster to the air.

Soon enough I reach the gates of the Arnaud family cemetery with its statues of women supple with grief. I'm drawn to the elaborate mausoleums, but the macabre nature of the statues makes me want to leave. I'm just about to do so when I hear someone stepping on brittle leaves.

A young woman in a blue wool coat.

Thank God, she's alive. She glows with vitality and breath.

She looks like . . . I gasp . . . like she could be one of my sisters. She has our shape of cheek and jaw. I approach her and watch as a faint pink tinges her cheeks. Her eyelashes flutter, and she looks like someone who knows she is being stared at. She raises a trembling hand to tuck a lock of hair behind her ear.

"Is someone here?" she asks huskily.

She senses me! It's been so very, very long since my spirit has registered with the living. "I am here," I say.

"Where are you?" She stares directly before her face, like a girl blinded by consumption. I step forward and take her hand.

Take means that my fingers pass through hers as she shudders and steps sideways.

"I won't hurt you," I say.

"Are you speaking? I feel sound but so far away."

"Yes, I'm speaking," I say loudly. I understand the depths of frustration Phoebe exhibits when trying to reach Tabitha. It's so hard to be so close and yet not penetrate.

"I've always heard the tales that this place must be haunted," she says to herself. "So I'm tricking myself into believing it."

I cup both hands around her face and pursue her as she steps evasively back. I press my palm to her forehead as if feeling for fever. I yank fruitlessly at her shirt.

"Do you feel that? And that?" I say. "It's not your imagination."

She flutters her hands around her body as if she's surrounded by a swarm of midges, and trots backward.

"Oh, you coward!" I call after her. My one chance at reaching a living human with corporeality and the power to help us? I'm not letting her go.

I follow her down the rows of stones, registering her sobs with a sick pleasure. *I'm* causing them, because she *feels* me!

"Whoa!" says Miles. He's intentioned next to me. "What's all this, then?"

"A ghost hunter," I say grimly. "And now I'm hunting her in turn."

"Good show," he says with a cocky grin. "And yet, let's try not to terrify her, shall we? I can try to gently blow in her ear." He had told me he had been able to puff enough to bend a candle flame once.

"Oh, do!" I say.

"Ah God, I feel like an idiot," she says. "If there's someone here listening, I'm Kate Darrow and I've written a book about the ghosts of England . . . but I've never actually seen one before. I'm an expert in a field I'm not quite expert in!"

My jaw drops. "She's a Darrow like me!" I tell Miles.

"She looks like she could easily be your sister," he says. "Things get more interesting here every day. I thought all your family was gone?"

"Indeed!" I say. "When everything here at the manor ceased, my family left. They were horrified at my role in everything."

"But you had no children?"

"No! Good Lord, what do you take me for? This Kate must be descended from one of my siblings or cousins. There were certainly enough of those."

Kate is continuing on with me, mustering her courage and wiping away her few tears. "I've felt the cold air on my face just now, and the strange stirrings of air as if someone is speaking, but from so far away. I can't truly hear. I could be a fool for standing here talking to the wind, but I must try."

"Try harder!" I shout at her.

"Gor, we need to send her to ghost-perceiving school!" says Miles. I stop short. How interesting to think that we could train ourselves to do so. When I was alive, I never saw a ghost, but surely they were around me.

Once again I clamp my hands on either side of her face like a strident lover. "Miss Kate Darrow, I'm your ancestor!"

"Oh God, I'm feeling it, I'm feeling something," she whimpers. "I'm scared but I want this so badly." She doesn't withdraw but stands there letting my hands brush her cheeks, smoothe her hair.

"It's true," I say an inch from her ear. "I'm here and I'm a ghost." Miles blows air into her face for good measure. I imagine how this would look to someone who could see the spirit world, two of us accosting her and the confused, terrified, and yet fascinated look on her face.

"I believe it," she breathes. "Let go of me while I count to three."

I instantly take my hands off her and her eyes go wide. When she reaches four, I again seize her. "Again," she says. We let go, she counts, we seize. "I'm not alone," she says wondrously. "I feel you and now I must try to see you."

I don't know how to help her with this one. I can't make myself more visible. We position ourselves in front of her as if she is taking our photograph. She looks so intently right at me that I begin to laugh at the absurdity.

"I begin to see a wavering," she says. "Like when dust motes float through the air."

"Thanks," mutters Miles. "We're dust to her."

"Ashes to ashes," I remind him.

"If I look to the side, I think I can see you better," she says. Miles and I exchange a triumphant glance. She addressed us as "you." She firmly believes! "It's like looking at a star," she continues. "If I look at it straight on, I can't see it. But if I look to the side, I begin to see the murky outlines of your . . . form. You're female, aren't you?"

"She better be looking at you," says Miles.

"Oh my God. Two shapes. There are two of you!" All her courage leaves her and she turns tail and runs. This time she runs full bore and I let her go. I can intention to her when she gets too far.

She pummels her way down the side of the manor. She's nearly at her car when Steven flags her down.

I clamp my hand to my mouth. *No.* Kate can't be his next victim.

"Hello!" he calls. "Are you all right?"

She slows to a trot. "Oh my," she says. "I . . . I'm so relieved to see you. I got myself quite scared over there in the cemetery."

"This place does have a certain ambiance," Steven agrees. "But it was all in your head?"

"I believe so," she says, gulping down air and laughing in sheer relief.

"So much for all the counting and the murky female forms," says Miles. "But I'm sure she would've seen my bulging musculature at some point."

"How can you joke?" I ask, trembling. "He's going to hurt her."

He blinks. "But it's broad daylight."

Steven walks closer to Kate. "What brought you out here?" he says.

"Oh dear, this is a terrible way to introduce myself. My name's Kate Darrow. I'm actually, funnily enough, the descendant of a servant who once worked here at the manor."

"Hello," he says uncertainly.

I walk up to her and shout into her face, "Get into your car and leave! He's a bad person!"

"I heard from my professor that they found swords here on the property," she answers pertly, without noticing me. "She saw word in the newspaper and rang me. She had been very kind and read an early draft of a book I wrote that mentions the estate, you see. So I drove over right quick. I'm so cheered to learn there's a family living here now!"

Steven looks nonplussed.

"Run, Kate!" I scream into her ear.

"Hold a bit," says Miles. "He's not going to do anything

to her right here in the courtyard. Maybe we can learn something."

"Oh, I know it's hard for you to tell that, isn't it?" says Kate. "The people of the village are never quite as enthusiastic as one might hope, are they? But disregard their frosty airs; I'm sure they're all delighted to have someone take an interest in the property again!" She's talking a mile a minute, so thankful to be away from the onslaught of "frosty air" I had given her, and talking to a living human again.

Steven manages to smile in the midst of this bombastic onslaught. "You're so kind to take an interest. Unfortunately, the household is shrouded in sadness now, which has overshadowed the excitement about the swords."

"Oh dear," she says. "Am I here at a bad time?"

"Well, it's more than just that," he says. "Several local teens have gone missing."

I gasp at his audacity in mentioning it. There's an unpleasant edge to it, too, as if he is cat and mousing her.

"Oh!" she says. Her eyebrows lift in surprise.

"Yes, the police are looking. We're hopeful the teens are safe somewhere. It's a large estate, as you know. Perhaps they became lost and are having trouble making their way out."

"He's quite a convincing liar," comments Miles.

"We should get Phoebe," I say. "Oh, Miles, I will not be able to stand it if he starts walking into the woods with her."

"Indeed," she says. "The land holdings here are extraordinarily large. It makes sense that they might've lost their way and have only to be found. It's not too cold at night; they'll be fine until they're located."

Steven breathes out, a lengthy exhalation.

"Miss . . . what did you say your name was?"

"Darrow."

"Miss Darrow, since you've made your way here with great excitement, I can quickly show you the site, but of course we have to stand at the cordoned limits."

"No!" I cry. "Don't go with him!"

"Oh shite," says Miles lowly.

"I'm so appreciative," she says. "How astonishing to be able to see the swords in situ from the medieval battle."

"Battle?" says Steven. "No, the archeologists have determined that the swords were laid in a ceremonial pattern. No skeletons with them, just the swords."

"Get Phoebe," I say, sick with dread. "Get her so we can get Tabby. Tabby's the only one we can use."

Miles vanishes.

"What pattern?"

"A circle."

Kate smiles. "How odd the men should all let their weapons go, at the same time. Makes one wonder if they all decided to get new ones at the same time. Sale at the armory!"

Steven chuckles, an odd sound I haven't heard much of from him. It sounds artificial. "Well, I'll show you the site."

Kate is an inspired conversationalist after her big scare and babbles all the while as Steven brings her round the side of the manor to the cache. I can't see Phoebe, Tabby, or their mum; they must've gone inside. How awful if they did. If they could just only turn the corner and see Steven with Kate!

Kate stands at the limits of the yellow tape and strains to see into the archeological pit. "How amazing," she says. "To think of so many other places all throughout England, where such treasures lie forgotten under the soil."

"It is a sobering thought," says Steven. "And so many of these things simply rot unburied. You say you grew up in Grenshire?"

I risk leaving him just for a second, to peek back around the side of the manor. No sign of anyone. I bite my lip and fight back tears, returning to stand next to Kate and take her hand. She's so involved in her discussion with Steven that she doesn't sense it at all.

"Please go, please go," I say in a choked voice.

I miss a bit of their conversation, but Steven continues questioning her.

"You mentioned the cold attitude of the villagers. It's almost as if they feared us coming across the very cache that we did."

She frowns. "How odd. I would think everyone would welcome the brightening of the manor. But I do recall that when I was researching my book there was a wall built across the drive, and I was deeply discouraged from entering the property."

"Did you regardless?"

"No," she says, smiling. "Bravery is not my strong suit. I relied only on oral histories for the chapter on the manor."

"So it is your first time visiting," says Steven. "Welcome to the place your ancestor once called home. And do you have brothers and sisters?"

In the midst of my terror, his reasoning registers. Steven knows it's important to be the firstborn.

"Many!" emphasizes Kate. "I fall in the middle, where my name gets occasionally forgotten."

"I'm sure not," says Steven. "It's fortuitous you are here. I've been trying to learn more about the manor's history, despite the locals barking me off." He pauses. "And just as you have a relationship through ancestry, so, too, do I. I'm an Arnaud come home."

I quell my trembling and focus on listening. Miles was right. We can learn from what he tells Kate.

Her eyes widen. "I had no idea any could still exist. Your family seems the stuff of legend."

"It seems my forebears were none too proud of our family name and fled."

"Odd, isn't it?"

"Tell me the focus of your book."

"Well. Please don't laugh, but my book is a collection of ghost stories from the British Isles. *Not At All Resting in Peace.* You wouldn't have heard of it." She waits, and I see that she wishes he would express knowledge of it. But his head is somewhere else.

"Do you see ghosts?" His eyes gleam, and the intensity of his desire makes my jaw drop.

Despite the evil he is capable of, he misses his daughter. He wants to communicate with Phoebe—and Kate Darrow may be the way to do that.

She blushes. "Well, despite my lifelong fascination with ghosts, I've never actually encountered one. At least not in a definitive, no-doubt-about-it kind of way."

"But you believe."

"I think so, yes."

"Ghosts are here," says Steven.

She smiles. "*You* see them, then?"

"I've seen my daughter. Sometimes her younger sister senses her." He pauses and I wonder if he'll explain about the Sangreçu.

"Your daughter is . . . ?"

"Yes. Very recently. She was sixteen."

"I'm so very, very sorry. I can't imagine your pain."

"My pain is a hundredfold knowing she's here and I can't talk with her. Please, won't you walk around the manor with me and see if you can perceive her?"

Dread again surges through my body. "No, Kate!" I shout into her ear. "No! No!"

I see she feels guilty refusing him. She began this interview in excitement for finally seeing the home she's imagined and written about, and has now been pulled into a darker, sadder duty. "Of course. I'd be honored to. In fact, I oughtn't say anything in case it was nothing, but before you came outside . . . I could've sworn I felt hands upon me. Icy palms upon my face. I was quite terrified, to tell you the truth."

"Don't go with him!" I scream. "Get in your car and go home!"

"Phoebe wouldn't do that," Steven says, frowning. "She wouldn't try to scare you."

"I don't believe the spirit—if it was one—intended to scare me, but only to convince me. It was extraordinary, really," she says. "And it scared me."

"When our loved ones pass, we are only scared for the realm they inhabit," says Steven. "My daughter is all right, although confused. She believes she and two others here . . . two other ghosts . . . are intended to fulfill some kind of prophecy."

I lower my voice, as if perhaps the hushed intensity might reach her when my shouting doesn't. "Kate," I say. "You must leave."

"There is a prophecy," says Kate slowly. "I included only a sentence about it in my book because there wasn't much to go on. I don't know the language of the prophecy, only that it has to do with Arthurian legend."

Steven puts his hands on his hips and shakes his head in disbelief. "Seriously? That is . . . well, it's preposterous. And my daughter is female."

"There were strong females connected with the Arthur story."

"Who?"

"Guinevere, Morgana, Nimue, to name a few."

I tug at her arm, trying to drag her away, but of course it is like pulling at air. "Miles!" I yell. "Come back!"

"We're far from Glastonbury Tor," he says, referring to the place where Camelot was thought to be.

"True, but there are many other places associated with the legend," she says. "The castle where the Grail was achieved, the site of the battle where Arthur fell—"

"These swords," says Steven, gesturing to them, half buried in the dirt. "Do they have something to do with Arthur?"

"I've no idea," she says.

"Then Excalibur would be in there!" Steven says excitedly. "The famous sword he pulled from the stone!"

"No," she says. "That was thrown back into the lake, remember? The lady's hand arose and caught it. But I do wonder . . . if they are arranged in a circle, are they the abandoned weapons of the knights of the Round Table?"

They stay silently looking at the dull glints of metal.

"What is my daughter's role?" he asks quietly.

Miles is back. "I can't get her," he says. I let out a sob. "There's trouble with her mum. She's found the—"

"Kate is so sweet, so vulnerable," I say. "I can't stand this."

"Listen, there's a lot going on at once," he says. He takes a deep breath. "I think Kate will be okay. Steven would be very bold indeed to do something to her right here."

"But if he convinces her to start walking," I say. "Then it's . . ."

I run out of words.

Miles looks at me, and our eyes communicate our incredible helplessness. It's one thing to meet a ghost after their death, quite another to see the person still living and feel unable to prevent their murder.

I break the gaze and look down at the swords.

"Why didn't they keep digging?" Miles murmurs. "They could find the others."

The sounds of the battle worm their way back into my head, growing in volume until I clap my hands against my ears. So much pain. A guttural roar from men who knew if they didn't kill, they would themselves die. A brutal choice. The clang of metal on metal and then a horrible softer sound as metal found flesh and bone.

"Look at me," says Miles suddenly. "It's different."

We stand on a remote grassy plain, nothing but stones and sky surrounding us. Clouds move swiftly, and I fall under the bewitchment of light and shadow capriciously alternating.

I stare into his face, so very well known to me at one time. I taught him all he knew.

He was a bewildered child before I trained him. I loved him as a son and fastened his hand around the sword, taught him the birdcalls to bring his falcon swiftly to his side. I cautioned him against usurpers, I hired a man to sip his wine and taste his food for poison. My proudest day was when Arthur regained the throne once stolen from him. I was his champion, his empire builder, his confidant, his rock.

I hated the hold Guinevere held over him, that foolish, fickle, lovely girl. She came between him and Launcelot, the most pure of men if not for her interference. And she was nothing! Powerless to the extreme, but for that pleasing arrangement of face and figure.

Tears roll from his eyes. "I know you now," he says.

"My guise is greatly changed."

"You changed endlessly," he says. "Why is it any different now?"

"My king," I say. "My beloved, dear king."

"And you my advisor, Myrddin," he says.

CHAPTER FOURTEEN

I've spent many rainy afternoons at the streaming window, tea in cup, trying to understand what has so compelled me on the topic of ghosts. I believe perhaps it is because they evoke our nostalgia for a life we didn't live . . . or a life we lived but don't recall. The Victorian wraith in the forlorn hallway, embittered by her own murder, may simply by her dress and adornments offer an alluring familiarity to me because I, too, once wore such garments.

—From *Not At All Resting in Peace: Ghost Stories of England, Scotland, and Wales* by Kate Darrow

*M*y cheek against his shirtfront, and I remember a rougher fabric back then, the cambric spun by the ladies at the fire. What a different world back then. Simple to the extreme. Meat on a spit and rushes on the floor, and stone to keep out the wind. That was all we needed.

I hover, as he does, in the remembrance of the past and the complexity of today. Sometimes I look down and see my black servant's gown, and sometimes I see the dyed linen and samite.

"The day I visited the cottage, when I overheard them say, 'I believe we are very close to finding mirth and . . .', I thought there was more to the sentence," I say. "But it ended in a period. They were saying, 'We are very close to finding Myrddin.'"

My ancient Welsh name, pronounced *mirth-in*. Books, many of them in the library at the Arnaud Manor, with garnet-eyed lions flicking forked tongues in the margins, recorded my name as *Merlin*.

"And Phoebe," he says.

A world of silence as I contemplate the complicated,

centuries-old, devastating guile of that woman. Not Guinevere. No.

Nimue.

"It makes sense she drowned in her last life," he says.

Yes.

Perpetually connected with water. One of the ladies of the lake, who sinuously came ashore and with her curls dripping wet, inveigled me. I was undone by the hue of her lips, moist eyes, the vague blue sheen of her skin in certain light. A weird sister from the depths who led me around by my previously dried heart, which she brought to life like a garden after rain. She spoke of the moon's sitting on the surface like a glowing orb that she would surface through, crowning herself. She had secrets, and she lured mine out of me, like a fisher at the edge with his line cast in. Eagerly I gave her all the power she needed to ensnare me in every possible way.

I was in love with her to the degree of madness. I couldn't spend an hour without wondering where she spent hers. I pressed too hard, and she showed her teeth. She was used to flickering away into the shadows of underwater caverns. My pursuit was, I now mark it, too aggressive.

I will not say I deserved the treatment at her hands.

No one deserves what she gave me.

"You disappeared," says Miles. "Back then. I didn't know where you had gone. I lost against Mordred because you weren't there to guide me."

I groan in deep agony. So much undone, because of one woman's betrayal. All the good of Arthur's Round Table, the men who brought order and purity to the rough kingdom, unraveled by her falseness.

"Where did you go?" he asks.

"She buried me."

★ ★ ★

Before I can begin to plumb these scattered, half-remembered memories, we are back at the manor. Kate and Steven are still standing at the edge of the pit of swords. I take a shaky breath of relief as I see Phoebe's mum come tearing around the corner of the building, pulling Tabby with her. Phoebe follows, her face grave. All I can think is, *Kate is safe.*

"Hello!" Steven hails his wife, but she doesn't respond.

Rage and deep, fundamental terror mottle her fair skin and make her eyes a fearsome blaze. She runs to him, out of breath, staggering with effort. Still holding her mother's hand, Tabby stands at her side and hugs her leg.

"You've seen the cemetery?" she asks him. She glances over at Kate Darrow and her face drains. She pushes at Kate. "Go home! Go!"

"Pardon me," says Kate as she regains her balance.

"Anne, the cemetery? Yes, of course I've seen it. You've seen it, too, I might dare add," says Steven in a reasoned voice. He puts a hand on his wife's arm, which she violently shakes off.

"*Not that one!*" she screams.

"What's going on, Phoebe?" I ask.

Phoebe's caressing her sister's hair for all it's perceived or not.

Miles answers for her. "Anne found the second cemetery."

So that's why he couldn't get Phoebe to come.

"I don't understand," says Steven.

"There's a gate in the back of the cemetery and you push through and then there's . . ." Phoebe's mum angrily wipes at tears on her cheeks with her free hand. "You, my dear, really ought to go home now," she says to Kate. She tries to muster up a smile. "I know I'm being terribly rude, but you may not know there has been a lot of trouble here recently."

"I want to help," says Kate. "I know about your elder daughter."

Phoebe's mum stares at Steven. "Who is this?"

"She just showed up," says Steven. "She's curious about the swords."

"And you told her about Phoebe?"

"She sees ghosts."

Silence descends as all parties try to figure out how to respond.

"I'm sorry if I've overstepped or come at a rotten time," says Kate finally.

"Listen, Anne, let's talk with this woman and see what she knows about the prophecy Phoebe was trying to tell us about."

"Do you *know* what's behind that gate?" Anne asks. "Phoebe told us about Madame Arnaud's story but, Steven, until you see the rows and rows and rows . . ."

"I've seen it," says Steven quietly, and I hear Phoebe give a dramatic and frightening inhale.

"You've seen it? Then you know this is not a place to bring children." She pauses, and incredible torment etches her face. "Steven, *why are we here?*"

She takes a step back from her husband, and without seeming to realize it, turns her body so it looks like she's shielding Tabby from him.

He winces. Phoebe kneels next to Tabby and closes her eyes as she hugs her without substance.

"Steven?"

He gives a growl of frustration. "You know why we're here! Phoebe died!"

"But if we wanted to start fresh somewhere, why here?" She leans over and picks Tabby up. "I don't know what to think anymore. You're not the same."

Good for Anne. It seems like she's accusing him of having something to do with the missing teens.

"Of course I'm not the same!" he roars. "My kid is dead!"

She backs up, cowed by his anger. Similarly, Kate quietly turns and starts walking away.

"Don't yell at me!" Anne says. "Do you see I have a child in my arms? You're scaring her."

"I'm sorry," he says, but still in a loud tone. "Sorry, Tabby."

"Steven," Anne says in a small, persistent voice. "Why are we here?"

"I don't know! It seemed like a good idea at the time. We were paying taxes on an empty home. England seems safe, different . . . and don't lay this all at my feet. You agreed. You liked the idea of an eighteenth-century manor that needed attention."

"I wanted to bury myself in a project, yes," says Anne in tight tones. "But not in a place that's dangerous."

Kate opens her car door and looks over at the tense altercation. Limply, she raises a hand to wave good-bye, but no one sees her but me. "We're losing our best resource for understanding things," I mutter to Miles.

"So go with her," he says.

I pause. I can always intention to her, and I desperately want to see the outcome of this confrontation. We know Steven loves Phoebe, but was his motive for moving the family to Grenshire not a clean one?

"Don't worry," says Miles abruptly. "I'll keep an eye on

Steven, and I'll come get you if we need you. Go, see what Kate does."

"All right," I say. I take one last fleeting look at Phoebe entwined with her sister and mother, yet unseen by either.

And then I intention into Kate's car as she makes a quick turn in the cobbled courtyard and heads back down the long Arnaud drive. "Holy ghosts of Britain, I didn't see that coming," she mutters to herself as whatever she's doing creates unpleasant, grinding sounds from the motor.

Kate drives for an hour. I hold back from touching her, terrified at the speed at which we're traveling. I don't want to distract her in this important work of keeping herself alive. There are so many other cars around, and we travel at a pace that makes the roadside trees a green blur. I begin to feel dizzy. Is it possible people travel like this every day? As we pass other cars going our direction, I crane over to see their expressions. They evidence no fear. They're used to this.

Kate leaves the fast road for a slower one, and drives through a town at a more modest rate. I'm relieved. We pass stores and churches, which give way to homes. Kate does some clever backward trick to get us into a line of cars at the side of the road.

I smooth down my black gown, marveling again at the loss of my apron. I'm a whole other person without it. She turns off the motor, and I lean my head back, exhausted.

She enters a brick house with an interior stairwell. At the top are two doors with numbers on them, and she uses her key to open the one with the number three on it. I gather this building has been divided into separate living spaces.

Kate puts on a kettle; I'm happy to see her sensibleness in taking tea after such an ordeal. She crouches between a set of drawers made of metal and pulls out the bottom drawer. Inside are tightly fitting papers, divided here and there with stronger beige paper with arching bits that stick up. On them she has written titles. She pulls out the one that is called "Arnaud Manor."

She sits at her kitchen table and flips through the papers inside. She makes a satisfied sound when she finds a page that looks like one from a book, rather than handwritten. I'm not sure how she has this; it appears to be a copy. This is created of technology not available to me when I was alive.

As I lean over her, I realize it's actually a copy of a page from Steven's secret societies book. I reel.

There must have been more than one copy. She said she hadn't been to the manor before. So somewhere in a library there must be another.

In the margins, Kate has previously written out translations for the Old English words. "Let's put it all together," she says. She opens a computer sitting on her table and begins to type the handwritten notes in.

She pauses now and then to pull out her phone and check a word again. I begin to exult as I watch the words appearing on the screen, now comprehensible. This is the translation Raven Gellerman and her group should have made. We would've known more, earlier, if they had.

Kate types, "On a strand the king does slumber, and below the meadow the dragon battle." She pauses and I see her handwrite in her notebook next to the word *bataille*, "noun rather than verb?" and she returns to her laptop. "The dragon battles the wicked trap with scorn from the damsel, and the goodness undone for she who betrays. But if you seek those of the same likeness and lineage, for a long time tolerate to come thereby the three people born on the day of such clamor for the king . . ."

She writes in her notebook, "day of clamor? Clue?"

I am hugging myself with fierce glee. This is about us! We are the three people born on the day Arthur fell.

She continues typing, ". . . and have them drink of Sangreçu blood . . ."

"Whatever that is," she says aloud.

". . . then they may learn the hiding places and bring the lost to might, once again will Britain arise to her glory."

So that's it.

All three of us have to drink the Sangreçu blood. Phoebe's treachery in drinking my portion has landed us here in this wretched halfway station. I have to find the vials and drink to enact the last part of the prophecy: learning the hiding place and bringing the lost to might.

I'm the hidden one, buried by Nimue, and Arthur is the lost. His return to power will again bring England to glory.

Where am I hidden? Where did that traitorous wench Nimue put me?

CHAPTER FIFTEEN

Were the incubus and succubus invented to explain the surprise
of climaxing while one sleeps? Or, further, to shift blame away
from the wanderings of restless fingers in the night? They are
said to be demons—the incubus a male preying on female
humans, and the succubus the reverse.

—*Demons & Angels throughout History*

I intention back to Phoebe.

She's inside the manor with her mother and sister. Steven is nowhere to be seen. Tabby is watching a show on the telly while her mother stonily stares at the screen without truly watching it. Phoebe is sitting with her face in her hands. She isn't moving.

Miles intentions into the room immediately; he must've sensed me coming. "Did you learn anything?"

"I did," I say grimly. "We all have to be Sangreçu to face our next task."

His face splinters into regret mixed with anger. He had tried to keep a few drops for me.

"How do you know that?"

"Kate sat down and very handily translated the prophecy. Something anyone could've done. So why didn't Raven?"

"Or Steven," says Miles. He whispers the next part so Phoebe won't hear. "Anne has kicked him out. She's scared he brought her and Tabby here for malevolent purposes. The door's locked hard against him."

"So where is he?"

"He's just thrashing through the forest. I've been follow-ing him for the last hour. I'll go back again immediately."

"Do you think Anne is right?"

He glances guilty over at Phoebe. "Come with me," he says.

We intention to the late-afternoon woods, where Steven is using a tree limb to smack at anything in his way, tree trunks, boulders, to express his anger. He's walking like he can barely stand to be in his skin.

"Not an easy man to have a word with," I say.

"No. He's off the deep end. And so was his wife."

We watch him. His branch splinters to the degree he throws it in the underbrush as hard as he can and then rakes his nails into the bark of the nearest tree.

"He's unhinged," I say.

"But he seems to truly love his children."

"He may be in the influence of larger forces. Just like us."

"So, we have to find another vial for you, and that's the number one job, you say?" says Miles.

"That's what will allow my former self to be found and your former self to be revived. Out on your island of Avalon, which you can doubtless see from the beach you and Phoebe tend to like to visit."

He smiles gently. "It all went so wrong, didn't it?"

"With you and Phoebe?"

"Yes. And with the three of us back then. I can't remem-ber anything but the swords flashing and the blood on the grass, but I understand from history that the kingdom of Camelot was very well received."

"Indeed. It will be a pleasure to reestablish it," I say.

We both laugh, his ringing a bit more like a snort. "It is ridiculous to think of, isn't it?" he says.

"It's all been ridiculous," I say.

"A few months ago I was just a guy on the swim team."

"A few centuries ago I was just a servant carrying a tray."

"And what was Steven?"

We look ahead where he's trampled a path through the forest like a questing beast. He's not one of the three, but is he something?

Hours later, as darkness begins to sidle into the woods, Steven sinks to the forest floor and curls up on his side. He pulls leaves into his fists and crushes them until his breathing steadies and we understand he's asleep. Miles and I hover over him, unsure what to do.

"Do we think he's guilty?" Miles asks.

"I think he wasn't strong enough to fight off the evil," I say.

Miles nods slowly. "Poor Phoebe," he says.

"And Dee and Alexander and Amey," I remind him.

"I know, I know," he says. "Seems like someone should just burn this forest and tear the manor down."

"I have no objections," I say.

"Speaking of Phoebe . . ."

Irritability courses through me. She's all he ever thinks about. He's about to ask me to stand guard over Steven, so he can go see her. So before he can ask, I say, "I agree. I'll go see her. You stay here and watch Steven."

His mouth opens to form a protest, but without waiting to hear it, I intention back to the manor, where Tabby's mum is reacting to knocks on the front door.

"Is that you, Steven?" she calls through the wood. "I'm sorry, but I just need some time to think about things."

"No," comes a female voice. "It's Kate Darrow. I've come

back, and I think I have some good research to share with you."

"No, thank you," she calls. "Busy day here for us."

Silence.

"I was here earlier. I was talking with your husband."

"You were?" Tabby's mum frowns. She's in such a state she doesn't remember who Kate is.

"I know about your elder daughter."

At that, Anne undoes the locks and opens the door. "Come in quickly," she breathes. "My husband's out there and quite angry."

Startled, Kate comes in, and Anne redoes the locks behind her.

"Have you seen my daughter?" she asks starkly.

I turn and look at Phoebe, who shakes her head and rolls her eyes at the same time.

"I might have done," says Kate. "Before your husband saw me, I was standing alone and could have sworn I felt cold hands on my face. And then, as I tried so very hard to see the entity, I could see two forms."

Phoebe's mum breaks into incredulous laughter. "My God! It could have been her! And that boy!"

"I believe so. One shape seemed clearly female but the other had a more hulking substance. In fact, I turned tail and ran when I realized there were two. I wish I had stayed and tried to learn more."

"Dear girl!" says Phoebe's mum. She reaches over and hugs Kate, who makes a noise of surprise before she hugs back. "Sorry, such an American thing to do. But it moves me that you may have seen my Phoebe."

"Thanks, Eleanor," says Phoebe quietly. "It wasn't me, but if it means something to her, that's all that matters."

I nod soberly as I watch Phoebe's mum try hard to master her desire to break down crying.

"My younger daughter, Tabby, is asleep, so we can talk without her interrupting. You said you brought some research?"

They sit down at the kitchen table, and Kate pulls the translated prophecy pages out to show her.

"It's all happening," says Phoebe. "It just took someone who was really invested in figuring things out. Unlike . . ." her voice trails off.

I don't dare look at Phoebe. Steven was never trying to find out the truth. He had turned away Miles's parents. He hadn't truly spent time in the library searching for the books that could help. He had fostered the appearance of looking, by leaving books on the kitchen table for us, open to certain pages, but he hadn't managed to find what my Kate found in just a few hours of serious work.

"I don't know what this Sangreçu is," falters Anne. "But it let her come back to us, talk to us. Very briefly."

Kate nods. "That is a powerful force."

"And cruel. It wore off."

"Imagine its force had she drunk while alive," says Kate.

Phoebe makes a tiny sound, and I again resist the impulse to look at her. It would be unkind.

Tabby's mum slumps forward, her face blanching. "I hadn't thought of that," she says.

"I'm sorry," says Kate. "I hope I didn't say the wrong thing."

"There is no 'wrong thing' for me now. Please don't worry. My whole system of what is upsetting has adjusted," says Tabby's mum. She sits back up and appears to make an attempt to square herself up. "It seems like the three people in the prophecy are probably my daughter and the two friends she told us about."

"Perhaps so," says Kate. "There's so little information about the Sangreçu, and none of it online. I had to return to the archives where I found the book in which this prophecy appears. I combed the shelves, scanning the texts. I only found a few mentions."

"Thank you for all your efforts on our part."

"Are you ready for some really 'out there' information?"

"Yes," says Phoebe at the same time her mother says, "I think so."

"It's Christianity meets King Arthur," says Kate. "Did you know Launcelot was an eighth-degree descendant of Christ?"

Anne looks at her blankly.

"I know, it's so silly sounding. The man of a myth connected to a historical personage."

Anne wipes her forehead with the back of her hand and seems to be rousing herself to some better form of interest. "So much of Christian history has its roots in pagan lore. The Christmas tree, the Easter bunny."

"Exactly so!" says Kate. "And it is said Merlin was the child of a Christian princess and an incubus."

"A what?"

"A sort of demon that visits in the night for sexual purposes."

"And can . . . impregnate?" Anne asks in horror.

"Apparently so."

"Really!"

"Birth control is so important," Kate says, venturing a joke, and is rewarded by Anne's surprised guffaw.

"You're too much!" They share a genuine, amused—

and might I say, *fond*—look. It crosses my mind that Kate is really not that much older than us . . . and given that Phoebe should be a year older now . . . is Anne relating to her as she might've related to a slightly older version of Phoebe?

"Merlin—actually, I should call him by his Welsh name Myrddin—has often been associated with dragons, as if incubi were not enough to have the mind reel," says Kate. "It's for that reason that the Sangreçu emblem . . . Sangreçu means *blood received*, by the way . . . is usually depicted as showing a trapped dragon."

"Because Merlin was trapped by his lover," says Anne. "I remember that from some movie."

I take a deep breath, or what passes for a breath postmortem.

"Yes. Merlin created the Sangreçu blood." Kate pauses. "Collect yourself?"

"Impossible, but please go on anyway."

"Sooo . . . the Sangreçu blood derives from trace amounts left in the vessel Joseph of Arimathea collected Christ's blood in. Commonly known as the Holy Grail."

"The Holy Grail," repeats Anne faintly.

"The Grail itself was achieved by certain knights of the Round Table. Men pure of heart, including Launcelot's son. That part of the tale is done. But Merlin took the most infinitesimal droplet, merged it with his own blood, said spells, and created a concoction that bestowed a sort of immortality on those who drank it. They can never die a blood death, although they can die other ways."

"So my daughter drank this blood and that's why she's haunting us? How did she get it?"

"I don't know. If she's one of the 'thre wyghts' from the prophecy, it would explain her lingering. The prophecy makes it sound like if she hasn't, she *should* drink. All three of them should."

"And how does a ghost drink?" Anne demands. She stands up and pushes her chair in, then thinks better of it and sinks down again. "I'm sorry to snap at you. It's all so much to take in, especially when teens are disappearing and I'm worried my husband—" She cuts herself off.

"You're worried about?"

Anne twists the wedding ring on her finger a few times before answering. "To be blunt and brutal, I'm worried my husband is involved in those kids disappearing."

Kate's jaw drops. "How you can think it?"

"The police think so, too," says Ann defensively.

"But he's so . . ."

"I know," says Anne. "I'm struggling with this, and I feel like a traitor for even thinking it. But he hasn't been himself."

"So can you keep an eye on him?"

"I can and have. As if I don't already have enough things to be concerned with. My daughter is dead, and she may well be listening now for all I know. I feel helpless and angry . . . and meanwhile my husband . . . I don't want him to harm anyone."

Kate nods. I venture a glance at Phoebe. She's looking at the surface of the table. I know she senses me, but doesn't look up.

"I feel sorry for you," says Anne. "All you meant to do was see some swords."

After Anne shows Kate to the door, she goes to look in on Tabby.

She sings a lullaby although Tabby's already asleep, and

then sits in the rocking chair crying softly. The power of her lonesomeness is fearsome to me. She can't trust her husband, her daughter is dead, she's trapped in a manor with a gruesome history, and now she's been told absurd and preposterous stories about how her daughter might've drunk a potion whose root is Christ's blood.

"Mom, no," says Phoebe, kneeling beside her.

I feel I'm violating their very private grief. "I'll come back later," I say softly. She nods without looking up.

I intention to Miles, sitting with his back up against an oak, near the sleeping form of Steven. "He hasn't moved," he says.

"Do you want to go with me, then? Phoebe found a vials rack in the cellars. Empty, of course. But perhaps worth looking at again."

"Incredible," he says. "But there's no use for us to go without her, is there? It will be pitch-dark."

He's right. It is fruitless to go without her special power to touch older Arnaud materials.

"So let's go get her," he adds.

I tamp down my irritation. All he wants is her. "She's having some special time with her mother."

"No, she isn't. Her mother has no idea she's there."

"Well, she's . . ."

"It's the perfect time to act. Steven's dead asleep and can be left for a while."

I look down at Steven, his chest moving with his deep breaths. "He's exhausted."

"Exactly so. Let's fetch Phoebe. Where there's a vials rack, there must be vials."

★ ★ ★

After a brief discussion with Phoebe, we intention down to the cellars, where she locates another set of matches to light a torch for us. We return to the empty vials rack, lying sideways from when she threw it. Perhaps there's a clue we missed. I stare again at the elegant tracery, where glass bottles once dangled.

Did I slide the bottles into their metal housing? After I'd paid the silversmith for his work and dismissed him?

I do my best to access that shadowed part of my brain where some residual memory may lie. Apparently I created the mixture inside the missing vials, with traces of holy blood and my own conflicted, half-demonic blood. Did I make a hundred vials, or five? Where did I place them? Some were here, and some were in France.

Think, Eleanor. Remember. Throw yourself back through the centuries. Phoebe and Miles had remembered only fractured bits of images when they drank the Sangreçu blood. Miles saw himself on the battlefield, which surely must've been, based on his description, his last day fighting at Camlann.

I flush thinking of Phoebe's recalled memory. It was her burying me.

"I only hear the faintest fog of sound from the rack," says Miles. "Can you sense anything, Eleanor?"

"You're the only one who ever hears it, Miles," says Phoebe.

It strikes me that if Phoebe is of the water, he is of the air. He can blow the candle flame, he hears sounds none of us do.

And if that is the case, what am I? Of the earth? Of fire?

Of rock, I conclude. I can sense the rock above my head, the capstone that has kept me still as a statue. I am of caves, grottoes, dark places. Hardened dragon scales. Armor plates. Immobility.

It wasn't always so. I was the most mutable of beings. I shape-shifted. I became many men. I loved trickery of all sorts. Those of us who work spells delight in deception. In our nature is the desire to surprise, to make things not as they are. To cast a glamour on faces so they appear to be other faces.

I taught these things to Nimue.

I traveled the world in many guises. I was in France, the land that drew so many of the knights. I sidled through forests where only a few trees away a beast snuffled and snorted, unaware of me. I pulled gems from crowns and reappointed them. Pretending I was too lame to walk, I cast away my walking stick and crouched and sprang like a tiger. My favorite expression on another's face, the perpetual O of disbelief. And on Nimue's face I wished to make that soften, wished to see her neck arch like the swan's, wished her breath to catch in her throat for me.

I so carefully doled out those vials. I have one image now, which flashes in and flashes out, like a scene briefly illuminated by lightning. It is the remembrance of digging a hole for one vial alone, buried without the dignity of a special rack to hold it. I had asked our silversmith to make several racks, but then I also bent to the soil and buried a vial without one. Because I knew I was not the only one who loved trickery.

The wise baker always keeps back a loaf, they say.

"There's another vial somewhere," I tell Miles and Phoebe.

"Where?" she says.

I stare at her. She's part of the reason I had to hide it!

"Eleanor, what's giving you that feeling?" asks Miles.

I force myself to look away from Phoebe's lovely but trea-
sonous face. "I was thinking of rocks on top of earth."

And then with a sickening feeling, I get it. The giant
clawing his way out of the dirt. The statue at Versailles in
the Enceladus Grove, cast by a medieval artist who was part
of that silversmith's heritage, created in winking homage to
me. *I* am the giant, in power if not size, and I'm still underground.

We can't even think of Tabby for this. How could she pronounce *Enceladus*? And how could her mum even associate it
with a place at Versailles so briefly visited? No. We have to
try to reach Kate Darrow.

She's in her flat eating dinner with a tableful of friends.
She's telling them what happened to her, and they refuse to
let her be serious about it.

"Oooh, ghost shapes! Kate, finally you have achieved it!
You see dead people!" says one lad, toasting her with his
glass of wine.

"How lovely it blew in your face instead of rattling chains
and wailing. This is today's ghost, loving and affectionate,"
adds the woman to his side, wearing an ochre knit cap.

"It wasn't like that," says Kate.

"Now you can write a sequel: *Love Stories of the Living and
the Dead*," hoots another man.

"*Fifty Shades of Graveyard*!" says the first lad.

"Will you let me finish?" pleads Kate. "There's so much
more to it."

"Next time, please take me," says the knit cap woman.
"Won't you?"

Kate says nothing, cuts her chicken while she waits for
them to calm down. It takes a good while. I believe they

have already been partaking of the wine; their spirits are very high. But finally her somber nature is noticed.

"Ah crap, Kate, really?" says one of the men.

"I should throw you lot out," says Kate. "I feed you and you won't even listen to me?"

"I did bring the starter," points out the other man.

Kate throws her napkin at him and reluctantly smiles. "I've had a really intense day, haven't I? There's really, truly something going on at the Arnaud Manor. The wife is worried the husband's abducting people, and indeed people have gone missing. I listened to the radio on the way home and they were talking about it."

They look at her, laughter fled. "Well, then, love, you mustn't go back there," says the knit cap woman.

"But I feel I have to. I helped the wife out with some research, and I just . . . I know I can't even talk to you about it, you'll start making fun again."

"We won't!" the woman protests.

"Oh, but you will. What matters is that I can be there for her as someone who believes. I'm planning to go back there tomorrow."

"Don't get yourself into something odd, Kate. This house is in the middle of nowhere, you said, and someone's a psychopath!"

"Wherever did you get that from?" Kate asks in amazement.

"Well, isn't the husband killing the missing people? And eating them with a nice Chianti?"

The table dissolves into laughter again. "Seriously, Kate, if you feel you have to go, please don't go alone. Bring one of these strapping lads with you," she says.

"Cor, nice to see that you don't volunteer yourself!" says one of the men.

There's too much commotion to try to reach Kate, so we wait until after dessert, until conversation dwindles down and finally her friends retrieve their sweaters from the back of the sofa and hug her good-bye.

She clears the plates and puts them in the sink. She pulls out her papers again to study the notes she made earlier.

"Blow out the candle, Miles," I urge.

We're lucky the crew lit a taper to eat by. Miles leans over and briskly blows the candle out.

"Oh, bother," says Kate. She continues reading. It's a funny thing how long it takes the fact to penetrate. She looks up at the candle, then at each of her windows, closed to the nighttime air. "Oh," she says softly.

"Light it again," I urge her.

But she doesn't. She sits, looking around her as if burglars and criminals are crowding each other to get to her.

"She's terrified," says Miles.

I pause, my hand extended to her cheek. "Do you think I oughtn't touch her?"

"Maybe give her a few minutes first. She really does look freaked out. It's probably one thing to see a ghost when you're in a cemetery, and quite another when it's in your own kitchen."

I put my hand down and study her face.

"Is someone there?" she asks.

"It's us," says Miles cheerfully. "We came to you this time! Special delivery."

"We are the very, very nice ghosts who mean no harm and are not malevolent," I say.

"Did we already mention nice?" says Miles.

I wait for her eyes to stop shifting around the room and focus on my shape. It takes a while.

She gasps. "I see you! A sort of wavering of the air!"

"Yes!" I say. "Well done!"

"Now try to listen to us," says Miles. "Take us to the Enceladus Grove, where you've got to do some digging and find us some Sangreçu blood."

I look at him. "She can't possibly take all that in," I say. "Maybe let's start just with a word."

"Enceladus."

"That's too grandiose," I say. "How about *help*?"

Over a period of hours, we work with Kate. She's an easier target than Tabby once she manages to calm down. She puts her pencil to the paper and writes down key words as we make them clear to her.

There has been so much shouting into her ear that my throat is sore. Miles has gotten so worked up he had to leave for a bit, but then came back. I don't stop for a second. By the time we finish, a sliver of moon is at the window listening in.

"All right," says Kate. "Looks like I have a little sudden vacation in my life."

Chapter Sixteen

The grounds at Versailles were constantly reconfigured. For instance, a hedgerow labyrinth with thirty-nine fountains with statues based on the Aesop's fables animals, positioned to appear as if they were talking to each other with water spewing from their mouths, was replaced a hundred years later with an English-style garden. The estate is a jigsaw puzzle of projects begun, abandoned, completed, destroyed.

—*Nooks and Crannies of Versailles*

A day later, Miles and I are in the Enceladus Grove again, the little walled garden on the grounds of the palace of Versailles. Phoebe's back in Grenshire alternately watching Steven and her little sister. The statue of the giant is so upsetting, so majestic in its uproar. He holds a stone he has clawed his way to the surface with, but there is no one to throw it at. Did he ever get revenge, I wonder?

Kate has brought a garden trowel that fit in her purse, and she takes it out now as she regards the statue contemplatively. There are about six other people here in the trellised grove with us. She can't exactly kneel and start digging; she'd be reported.

She walks around the circular limits of the fountain. "Do you know where I start?" she asks the air—which means us.

"I don't know," I answer, but I know she doesn't hear me.

"Wouldn't they have found the vial when they built the fountain?" asks Miles.

"The sculptor knew," I say. "He was Sangreçu, too."

"And you know this how?" he asks.

"The way you know you fought with a sword and watched your own blood spill to mar the green field."

"Convincing enough," says Miles.

Kate sees something we don't, gasps, and bends to dig. We wait, hovering behind her to see what arises. She has to stop whenever people enter the grove. She keeps pausing, pretending to scroll through photos on her phone, until they leave.

It takes forever, and I can tell even she is getting frustrated, but finally her trowel hits something. She carefully pulls it out. Good timing, too: a few tourists have just entered the grove. She rises nonchalantly and walks away from the statue.

She holds a crumpled package, which looks to be a bed cloth folded over onto itself several times. "It's samite," she says to herself, and then for our benefit, "the fabric of royalty."

I look at Miles and see he is in a near swoon, his eyes drifting closed and his mouth open in a slackened ecstasy.

"You hear something?" I ask.

"Something? *Everything*! You can't hear that?"

"No."

I wish I could. Whatever enchanting song the blood sings, I wish I were listening to it. How unfair such gloriousness is only for him. I made the vials in some guise, some personage . . . and he experiences them better than I do.

Kate walks, and I don't even pay attention to where we go, so focused on the vials and what they offer me. She crouches behind a hedge to provide secrecy for us.

She delicately unwraps the folds of fabric until it's exposed to us, the small glass bottle with a cork at its top.

Miles groans and falls to his knees, his arms around his head to cover his ears. "It's too much," he says.

Kate's face. She is pulled to the vial. I will have to be careful or she'll take it all. Miles told me how it just has to tilt enough for a drop to land on your lip, and then it's yours.

Kate removes the cork and Miles cries out.

I see it in Kate, what had happened with Phoebe. Greed kicks in. That vial is meant for me—she knows it.

We're here only because *I* need to drink. No one else. It's all for me, and yet Kate is tilting the vial toward her own face and opening her mouth in anticipation. I hurl myself into the same space as her and uplift my face just as the bottle tips in her hands to deliver a sweet and succulent drop.

It lands on my lip the same time that it lands on hers. We are aligned and we each taste. We become Sangreçu at the same moment.

I pull aside the bed curtains. Fire flickers at my back. The moon in the casement is large and ominous over the sea. Nimue and Arthur make love, so involved in each other they don't notice my presence.

How my heart shrivels in that tower room, so secretive for the clandestine lovers, while Guinevere sleeps downstairs, while Nimue supposes me off on a voyage I'd failed to take.

Everything stops for me. She is beautiful as I knew she'd be, her body lush and willing, her hair winding around her and around him and unwinding to the floor as if still coming from her head. Magic is making her more fertile and growth-filled; longer nails now clench at his body.

I wanted this for myself, and she gave it to Arthur.

I howl at the betrayal, and the lovers cease. Her green eyes panicked and sorrowful and gloating, all at the same time.

I am filled with nothing but Nimue. She was all I wanted.

She was my every breath and my every thought, from the day I met her.

I hear her voice whisper, "I'm sorry" as I hurtle back to Miles and Kate.

"I saved some for Phoebe," says Miles in a slurred voice.

"How lovely your first thought is of her," I say tartly.

I know where I am. That witch, that circular-spelled siren buried me deep, and the Arnaud Manor was built upon my hiding place. It was known and then forgotten. The protectors kept the prophecy spoken of, and they waited for me to be found. Today at long last, I will roll back the capstone and release myself.

"Eleanor?" asks Kate, and I see her eyes widen at my appearance, her first time seeing me. I don't bother to answer.

I use intention. They don't need to know where I'm going. It's all my quest now. They can take the plane flight back to England, since even as Sangreçu, the living Kate can't use intention. But I can't wait. I'm heading to Rookmoor.

The museum appears to be closed today, the lighting dim and no one around. I approach the chair, resting in its alcove. Some throne, made of flimsy wood and its embroidered seat, but it harks to far older than the Arnaud household. I climb over the velvet rope barricade, but my body, so unused to responding to the dictates of my mind, clumsily lurches. I fall, and the metal stanchions holding the ropes up clatter noisily to the ground. If there is a watchman, he is surely running to me at full bore.

I stand up and laugh. I actually feel *bruised*. My palm is stinging from catching my weight. It's a glorious sensation. "Catch me, I don't care!" I yell to the museum. "I will fight you off! And woe to the man who thinks he can best me now!"

I come to the chair. So many memories, and they roar through me at an awe-inspiring speed. It was Guin's chair, and so often as I conferred with Arthur, its charming air would play as she smiled at us. She was a sweet lady, it is true, although history has recorded her as a terrible wench who cuckolded Arthur. But truth be told, she was only doing to him as she was done unto.

I perch on it, and lo and behold, my body has weight and heft and the chair plays again. Tears stream down my cheeks for the power of that melody. Why is it that music holds us in such thrall?

When the song is done and silence lingers, I crouch at the chair and dig my nails into the embroidered covering and rip. I'm like a dog worrying a bone, and the sound of the ripping excites me, just as much as the music did. It is the sound of my body in motion and having consequences. Sheer joy in making things *happen* after so many years of muted existence!

My fingers dig and pull at the stuffing inside, creating clouds of snow behind me as I toss it. Inside is a magicked key, small and golden and powerful. So tiny it could rest on the tongue and be unseen as a woman tells lies.

The key to the capstone.

A stone can't have a key, but this one does. The membrane of a rock can be made permeable. A few choice words from necromancy and the solid becomes molten. This is how a sword can be lodged in a stone.

I take a flashlight from a drawer in the Arnaud kitchen and move to the cellars. I don't need Phoebe and her lucifers. My footfalls on the rough floor make me delirious with appreciation. Do the living even know how wonderful it is to hear evidence of your progress as you walk through your life?

Phoebe's likely somewhere upstairs. I don't care. I have only one task on my mind.

I go straight to the sacrificial table. It had nothing to do with the creation of the Sangreçu vials. It was a rudimentary altar for those who worshipped the woodland deity, that is true, but I had only knelt for that power briefly.

Beneath it, however, is a round and flat stone. We had missed it last time. Nimue had placed a spell on it so it could never be marked. No dragon emblem to call anyone's gaze, no runes to exclaim what lay beneath.

I apply the key to its surface and it sinks in, as if there is a lock there. I turn it clockwise and listen to the corresponding mechanism within the rock.

And then the rock shouts.

It isn't ready to give up its treasure.

I shout back at it. A grinding noise, and something revolves inside. A tiny bit of space appears beneath the stone as it raises ever so slightly. It is a hatch.

It takes all my strength to lift it. I try to remember a spell to make it lighter but I can't focus. Magic takes pity on me nonetheless and I feel the weight lighten.

I push the capstone to the side and look.

Below me, a well yawns. And taking up much of its space is a silver helm. And underneath the helm is the body of a man in full mail, standing upright. In the dim recess, his metal glints dully.

The air screams and the rock wails.

Your poisonous treachery is undone, my mind calls to her.

I claw down to reach him, to merge and blend with him,

myself, a different form of myself, fashioned in a different shape, poured into a different mold and yet me.

I lower myself into his narrow dungeon and press my face to the hard metal of his shield, held so futilely against his chest. His sword still at the ready but impotent against the worst of foes, the lover turned enemy who has all his secrets.

"Wake up," I whisper.

His face could be iron itself; he appears to be a statue.

I hammer on his mail with my fists and the tiny metal rings chink and clatter. "It's time to wake up!" I cry. I hit him, and all my aggression from the pains of every version of myself takes pleasure in battering him. Every slight, every insult, every bruise, repaid as I rain down anger and abuse.

It's not enough. Just finding him isn't enough.

I have to undo the spell.

And only Nimue can do that.

I find Phoebe sitting in the kitchen as her mom chops broccoli and Tabby makes a drawing at the kitchen table. She's overcome with sadness, I can see.

"You look different," she says.

"Come with me and release me," I command her. "I've found the hiding place, but can't undo your spells."

"How can I?" she says plaintively. "That was someone else. I don't have spells."

"Just come with me. Please!"

"I haven't checked on Steven in a while. I should do that before we go."

I hesitate. "Yes, all right," I say.

She rises and casts a glance back at her mother.

We intention to Steven. He's still in the woods, but his positioning is different. He is prone, side by side with a fallen log. His arm is slung over the mossy bark as if it is someone lying next to him in bed.

"How can he be still asleep?" I ask, frowning.

"Magic?"

I crouch and look at his face, unscraped and lax in sleep. Is the forest working an influence on him? Is he more vulnerable when sleeping?

"I wish we could stay here," I whisper. "But we have to go. I am *not* letting the Sangreçu effects fade without releasing Myrddin."

"I don't know what I can do," says Phoebe. "I don't know spells, don't remember anything. But I'll try."

"Of course you will," I say. Impatiently, I take her hand.

We intention to the depths of the cellars. I take us to the opening in the stone floor, where we kneel and peer down at the silent man in his helm and mail.

"Oh my God," she says in a raw voice, confronted by her own wretched act.

It is so dim and clammy here. We are underground, and the walls seep the earth's tears while the grotto keeps up an endless trickle. It is oppressively damp; I think it is the Lady of the Lake's centuries-old influence. She took the water out of the well and cast it to the walls.

He stands where once women cranked a pail on a rope to fetch the family's water. Never could they have dreamed a man would remain there, lost in his own thoughts, bewitched and tricked, for hundreds upon hundreds of years.

I can only hope he didn't understand his plight. Perhaps her spell even let him think he got what he wanted: her regard and love.

Phoebe turns her head so she can't see him any longer. "I warned you. I don't remember anything."

My fingernails curl on the stone floor. *She never does as I wish.*

My whole body shudders at the intensity of my nails scraping rock, such a small sensation. Colors, air: everything is so much richer when one is Sangreçu.

"Then you must drink again," I say.

"How can I drink?"

"Miles saved you some," I rise, wiping my hands on my gown. "It will wear off again as it did before. But this time, your first task is not to talk with your family. We understand the prophecy now. We have everything we need. We just need for me to be released."

"You *did* find a vial!" she says, her eyes wide. "I wonder why he didn't . . ."

I can tell my face holds a deep sneer for her. "Yes, you poor thing, you have been completely *betrayed* because he didn't race straight to you and chose to stay with Kate. Never mind that you saved none for me last time. Never mind that we are only in this state of inconclusiveness because of you! Because of your deeds and foul treachery!"

It feels exquisite to raise my voice and hear that most subtle of effects: an echo. Upstairs, Anne and Tabby might hear my speech ringing through the floorboards. It's extraordinary to feel spite color my cheeks. I'm furious . . . and it feels wonderful.

"Please don't throw in my face things that I did in another lifetime," says Phoebe.

"Why not? It was you."

"Not truly me."

"Selfish, cruel maiden," I say. "Although *maiden* doesn't really apply, does it?"

"You wanted my maidenhead," she says. "You were like a dog slavering after me. We're in this state because of *you!*"

"No!" I step back.

"Yes, you! You have blamed me all this time, but I had to put you in the ground before you killed me and killed Arthur! You were in a rage. You had put on your armor and challenged him to fight for my honor!"

I shake my head. Did I do that? The man we gaze upon wears armor, and I was so rarely kitted out that way.

"You were going to kill the king for jealous love of me. I couldn't have it . . . it would ruin the kingdom and all the good his rule put in place."

"No," I say again. But I am remembering my incredible, desperate sad anger that day.

"And then he was killed anyway, by his own son," Phoebe says. Her face shifts only for a second, and in that brief flash I see the ever so slightly different, lustrous face of magic-touched Nimue. "Fate will always out."

I've been so angry for so long. But was it fair to blame her? She fell in love. He fell in love. We can never control that.

"You pushed so hard," she says. "I didn't want your kisses, but you pressed them on me regardless."

I was despicable. And after everything we'd come to agree upon about the courtly treatment of ladies. The pillaging of burning villages—we had agreed not to take the women any longer, spilling our hatred into their bodies along with our seed.

"I am ashamed," I said. "And yet, I would've stopped, Nimue, at one word from you."

Tears roll down her face. "I had said 'no' before. You would withdraw and try again later. You never accepted my resistance, and when you found me with Arthur—you were filled with fury. I feared you would kill him and . . ."

Unspoken is the idea that she thought I would press her down and force her. I rebel at the thought, but she thought me capable of it. "So you cast a spell on me without waiting to see."

"I had so little time. You were so much stronger than me, physically and magically."

I hang my head. Perhaps this is my fault after all. I should've simply let the curtain fall when I saw them making love, returned to my quarters, poured my passion into heightening my skills to make Camelot stronger.

Instead, the kingdom fell. All those knights rode out to find the Grail, dispersing the Round Table. And when they wandered back years later with no stories to tell but grim ones, they laid down their swords in shame. That is the circle discovered by the bulldozer: weapons abandoned by the men who failed to wield them well. They laid them here where Arthur had died, then returned to live unpromising lives as craftsmen, bakers, smiths. All nobility erased.

"I am filled with regrets," I say simply.

"I want to release you," she says. "If I drink, I'll remember the words that bound you."

"It's unfair," I say, "how we are toyed with. I loved you so much, and you cared nothing for me. What cruel fate fashioned that for me, to love someone who scorned me?"

"I cared for you, just not the way you hoped. And please don't think I wasn't in just as painful a circumstance as you. The man I loved was bound in marriage to another woman and could never be mine."

"He was yours."

"His heart was mine, but was hers, too. He loved Guinevere, fiercely at one time."

"And she loved Launcelot . . . It is a wretched chain of failures."

I consider the ways we could've reshaped the past: Guin and Launcelot affianced, Arthur and Nimue, and me . . . alone.

CHAPTER SEVENTEEN

One wonders about place names and the secrets of the past they hold. For instance, *ham* means *farm* or *homestead*, so a town or street named Oldham is surely a place where an older home stood. Similarly, the lane in Grenshire that leads to the Arnaud Manor carries a name that indicates its earlier use: Auldkirk, which means *old church*.

—From *Not At All Resting in Peace: Ghost Stories of England, Scotland, and Wales*, by Kate Darrow

We intention to the backseat of Kate's car. She doesn't notice me, so intent on her wild driving. Miles is in front, and he, too, is so distracted he doesn't know we're here. Kate's traveling way too fast, weaving in and out between cars like a shuttle moved by a crazy weaver. She's laughing delightedly to herself.

Miles should be having a fearful reaction to the drive, but he's also recklessly enjoying the speed, waving at the inhabitants of every car they pass. "She saw me!" he exults. "She blew me a kiss!"

Everything on Sangreçu blood is drenched in color, drenched in emotion. Sensation is so expanded now for us who have gone so long without it . . . and I have gone longer without it than any of them.

Beneath me I feel the faded leather of Kate's seat, hear the grinding of her gears. The very motion of the car trembling beneath us. The smell of the gasoline, reminiscent of the kerosene we lit lamps with. I run my hands over my face just to feel my fingertips. I rake harder, then glide, barely touching. It is . . . beyond anything I can explain. It's my skin again. I am connected to it and sensation.

The motion of my arms moving above my head just to feel those muscles again, the sensation of stretching, that lovely tension: it makes Kate look to the mirror on her glass windshield and catch me.

She screams and wrenches her steering wheel so hard to the right that car horns blast at us and she pulls over to the side to regain herself.

She stops the car and sits breathing hard for a few minutes before she turns around to stare at me. She can't see Phoebe.

"My God," she says to me, her eyes open in stark shock. "You could be my sister!"

I smile. "I thought the same of you when I saw you. Do you know who I am?"

I watch her eyes move from my braid to my solemn black dress. "You appear to be have worked as a maid, it might seem?" she asks.

"Eleanor Darrow at your service, miss," I say.

It is so worth it to hear her sharp intake of breath and then see her hand clap to her mouth. "No!" she says.

I laugh, enjoying the burbling it creates in my throat. "Hello, Kate. Nice to see you again after our brief meeting in the cemetery. Phoebe is also here."

"I can't believe it!" says Kate. She extends a hand as if to shake mine, and I grasp hers in both of mine. So warm and sympathetic, that hand.

I am not ashamed to say that tears well up in our eyes.

"You're my ancestor," she says. "I'm looking at you. I'm . . ."

"Overcome?" ventures Phoebe, unheard by Kate.

"I'm so . . ."

"*Overcome* is actually the perfect verb," says Phoebe. "Take it."

"Shut it, Phoebe," says Miles, but somewhat kindly.

"I feel so much love for you," blurts Kate.

I surge forward and wrap my arms around her neck. We look, eye to eye, each feeling the poignance of seeing recognizable features. Maybe she has lost someone who looks like me. All my sisters are gone, of course, but it was Edie whose face in particular I see reflected in Kate's. "I feel the same," I say.

"Come on, Eleanor, tell her you love her. You might not've been able to in the eighteen hundreds but you can now," says Phoebe.

It is hard for me to talk about love. I don't think the word ever passed my lips in my lifetime except in church and Biblical scriptures. Even with Austin, I don't think we used such direct language. I look into the shine of Kate's eyes and muster my courage. "I must admit that I return your feelings of love," I am able to say.

Miles guffaws but Phoebe reaches over and squeezes my arm. And Kate . . . oh, Kate's reaction! The sunshine of her smile splinters my head apart.

"All right, I'd best get off the shoulder," she says as we unwind. "Not safe. And we've hours to go yet before we return to Grenshire."

"And we've a thirsty girl in the backseat," says Miles.

"Give it to me," says Phoebe to Miles, leaning over me to the front seat.

"May I present to you, dear Phoebe Irving, or perhaps and almost certainly *Arnaud*, the greatest and best of cocktails, only a drop of which is necessary for complete and total satisfaction?" Miles flourishes it like he is one of those medicine sellers who used to come to the kitchen door.

"You fool, you're holding it in your bare hand? What if you drop it?" she scolds him.

"We don't serve impudent customers," says Miles, withdrawing the vial from her.

"How can you even joke?" she says.

"I can joke because I'm feeling *fiiiiiine*. There's a lot of love in this car," he says.

"Fork it over," she says.

He gives it to her, and I watch as she tilts her long neck back. A single pendant of the blood comes off the glass lip of the vial, and she opens her mouth as if she's taking a large bite. It disappears into her mouth and she groans.

"Oh God," she says.

"Indeed," says Miles. "Hey, climb up front."

Phoebe's always been visible to me, but I watch the dawn of disbelief as Kate can now see her, too. "This is quite the day," she mutters to herself.

"You've plenty of material for a sequel, eh?" Miles asks her.

She practically shouts with hilarity. "You don't know the half of it," she says.

Brazenly, Phoebe crawls into the front seat and onto Miles's lap. Kate laughs aloud. "Hussy," she teases, and catches my eye in the mirror to wink. She pulls back onto the roadway while Miles and Phoebe kiss as if nothing could ever tear them apart again.

I turn my head to the side. I'm still thrilling to the world of feeling and touch, but there's a tinge of sadness seeing the lovers.

Austin. Why didn't I try to run away with him instead of taking my life?

"Okay, Miles and Phoebe, if you could remove your tongues from each other's epiglottis, let's figure a few things out," says Kate after a few minutes.

"No," says Miles.

"You get thirty seconds," says Kate. "PDAs are never pleasant for the others around, you know?"

"You get this all the time," says Miles.

Kate responds by driving faster, making the engine shudder. "I'm like a well-oiled machine," she says as she slides back into the lane between two cars with just a sliver of space between them.

"Phoebe," I venture. "Can we return and release Myrddin? See if you can remember the spell?"

"Wait—you found Myrddin?" Miles's face is an intense blaze.

"The Sangreçu helped me remember," I say, "which is why I wish it would help Phoebe remember. He is buried upright in a stone well in the cellars, a level below the old altar we found."

"I can't believe I'm just driving my car while all this is happening," says Kate. "I feel like I'm in a movie."

"He's just standing there?"

"Yes, with shield and sword," says Phoebe. "Rather pathetically prepared for a battle he can't fight."

She shares a glance with me. The battle was to have been with Arthur.

"Tell me about this altar," says Kate.

"It looks like a place where they sacrificed people," I say.

"There's so much yet to be learned about the pagan background of this area," she says. "You know the manor's address is Auldkirk Lane? That's a Scottish way of saying *old church*."

"So we are not only balancing Arthurian prophecies and our dismal deaths, but also pagan churches of an evil bent?" says Miles.

"Pretty much," says Kate.

"So, Phoebe, will you go with me?" I ask again.

"It will last until we get back," she says. "I want to be with Miles right now."

"Release Myrddin first, then come back and spoon with him," I say. "And don't forget, we have some bodies in the pond to . . ."

"Eleanor, don't tell me what to do!" she snaps. "I haven't felt this good in so long. I want to spend this time with Miles. Last time we were Sangreçu I blew it. I'm not going to blow it this time."

"Please!" I say.

She doesn't say another word, but the two of them intention away, leaving Kate and me alone in the car.

"What just happened?" Kate asks.

I can't believe Phoebe.

And worse . . . I can't believe Miles.

I consider intentioning after them, ruining their time together as lovers, but as angry as I am, I can't do it.

"Are you all right?" asks Kate.

I stubbornly turn my head away, watching the cars we pass and drifting into troubled thoughts.

They can satisfy their animal lust, and then I can only hope that Phoebe, newly endowed with Sangreçu blood, can stand next to Myrddin and remember what terrible spells she wrought to put him in that state.

When she and Miles return, Kate and I are already on the driveway to the Arnaud Manor. We've lost any head start we might've had. I refuse to talk to either of them. Kate pulls up into the courtyard and we get out, just like regular people, closing the car doors behind us.

CHAPTER EIGHTEEN

It is fundamental that when a servant has deliberately
disobeyed orders that he or she be made example of, so that
every other servant is informed of the misdeed and stands
witness to the punishment that of course must be severe and
of sufficient duration that each servant feels it as a stripe across
their own back.

—*Quelling Insubordination*

*M*y first thought, of course, is to go to the cellars, but Phoebe wants to check on Tabby first. I don't even bother to argue. I put on a stony face and we intention inside the apartment.

We arrive to chaos.

In Tabby's bedroom, Phoebe's mum is screaming and crying.

"Mom," says Phoebe.

Anne turns around with so much gratefulness in her face that it hurts to see it. "Phoebe," she says in a guttural voice. She seizes Phoebe and hugs her so tightly I'm sure in some way it hurts.

"What's wrong, Mom?" Phoebe asks.

"Tabby's . . . missing." A world of agony arises from that simple sentence.

Oh no. No. It can't be.

Anne dissolves into raw sobs again.

"It's okay, Mom, she can't be far," says Phoebe. "We'll look for her. I brought Miles and Eleanor and Kate."

Anne looks up and registers our presence, but just barely,

in eyes completely clouded with tears. "I've looked everywhere."

"Where's Steven?"

"I locked him out. As far as I know, he's still outside."

"But, Mom, you need his help to look for Tabby."

"No," says Phoebe's mum. "You're here, you all can help." I see her shudder although she tries to hide it. Of the five people in the room, only two are alive.

"How long has she been gone?"

"I was napping, and when I woke up I knew too much time had gone by but I never heard Tabby call for me," says Phoebe's mum, talking in ragged measure between sobs. "She wasn't in her crib."

"So then we look through the house for her, don't we?" asks Kate in an overly bright voice.

"It's just this one apartment," says Anne, "and I've been through every inch of it. She's either in the manor itself, in which case we'll never see her again, or she's out in the woods."

"Well, then, we'll look through the manor and call her name loudly. And then we'll head to the woods. She'll turn up, never fear," says Kate.

"Your optimism is ringing as ignorant and stupid rather than motivational," says Anne coldly, in between sobs.

Kate looks taken aback.

"I've lost a child, remember," says Anne, grabbing Phoebe's arm in a way that almost looks angry rather than loving. "And I know my husband is dangerous. What if he came into the apartment and took Tabby?"

I look at the floor. I can't bear to look at Phoebe's face. I kept her away from Tabby when she was trying to be vigilant. No one watched Tabby and her mother.

"I think I know where we should check," says Miles in a low voice.

He's probably right. The sacrificial table. The worst possible place for a child.

"Just give Mom a second to collect herself," says Phoebe.

I know it's selfish but I want to descend to the table for another reason besides saving Tabby. I want to station Phoebe in front of my inscrutable half-self until she remembers the spell to release me. We don't have all the time in the world. For the dead, the Sangreçu effects fade.

I try to recall spells of my own, so I can say them and trigger memories in Phoebe. It's astonishing how quickly they flood into my head once I try.

Welsh words, Gaelic, rudimentary syllables from around the primeval campfire. I say a few to her now, for her to hear the rough yet majestic sounds. She jolts, looks deep into my eyes. "I think I . . ." She whispers.

"Has this always been here?" asks Miles, interrupting. He's pointing to an oddity in the wallpaper. A seam has appeared.

No . . . no . . . Phoebe was just about to remember. I saw it in her face.

"It's just like the door at Versailles!" Anne cries.

Miles pulls, and a secret door opens, its outlines previously hidden in the busy pattern of the paper.

"She must have gone this way," he says.

"Gone or more likely taken," says Anne. "He knows this house. He's studied the blueprints. He must've snuck in and taken her."

"Mom, don't say things like that! It's Steven."

Miles is already in the passageway, crouching down be-

cause of its short height. I spy a child's flashlight in a wicker
toy bin and pass the lighted ladybug to him. I have to set
aside my own concerns for the sake of Tabby.

"Should we all go?" I ask.

It could be a trap, I say with my eyes. Miles responds, and
I flush with pleasure that we can again convey information
with our deep understanding as it was in days of old.

"Phoebe, you and your mother might stay," he suggests.
"What if Steven comes back? And surely you should call the
police."

Anne is torn. She wants to race down the passageway herself, no one faster than her when her child is involved. But
his suggestion does make sense; she's the only one who can
make that phone call and then talk with the officers when
they arrive. Seeing the face of the lad who died in a car accident, whose photo was likely plastered all over the newspaper, will cloud our cause. So, too, will someone dressed as
a nineteenth-century servant, or in Kate's case, a complete
stranger whose visit to the manor could be seen as suspicious.

Anne and Phoebe stay back while the three of us enter
the passageway and begin running. We leave a sweet, wall-
papered nursery and enter a dark stone passage. I've always
hated small, close passages like this, the tiny wine caves
and tunnels under thoroughfares to protect on rainy days.
But despite my anger at Miles and Phoebe, because of the
Sangreçu blood I revel in every musty stink it offers, every
rough rock surface my arm abrades if I tip off-balance from
the uneven dirt flooring.

It seems the walkway slopes downward as we go, and I
wonder if we are going to the cellars. Soon, I'm out of breath
from running. I feel myself grin despite everything, even if

the unsavory object of our mission hasn't eluded me. I like being out of breath. Phoebe and Miles taught me to like it at Versailles, running along the banks of the Grand Canal. I almost think I should never like to sit again, if I could always feel this marvelous hitch of my own breath.

The slope of the passage deepens until it's undeniable we are descending. "Tabby!" Miles calls ahead, as if she's done nothing but gone exploring what lay behind an open door. She did that once before; it's possible she's done it again, although my heart tells me there's more to it than that.

Abruptly, we spill into a cavernous room. I've never been here before. A tiled plunge sits in the middle of it. The water in it is dark as coffee.

"A swimming pool?" says Miles.

"Quite an innovation at the time, I'd say," says Kate.

"Especially for a mistress who didn't know how to swim," I say darkly. We walk around the edges of the room, trying to discern where the passage continues, or if this is a dead end.

Miles swears.

He bends over and picks up a teddy bear at the edge of the pool.

"Oh my God," says Kate in a tight voice. "Please, God, no."

We look at the dark surface of the plunge, its surface slightly rippling. The water has been recently disturbed.

"I'll go," says Miles.

"Phoebe drowned," I tell Kate. "This can't happen again. It just cannot. The world is not so cruel."

"Anne will kill herself if Tabby drowned," says Miles matter-of-factly. He jumps in and is gone. I crouch at the side and put my hand in. The water is somewhat warm, but what device heats it?

Miles surfaces a few times and then disappears for a longer while.

"He's okay, isn't he?" Kate asks me.

I stare at her, too exhausted to frame an answer that will allay her fears.

He surfaces near the wall. "There's an underground tunnel," he says. "It's short. We can do it."

I glance at Kate. I'd rather use intention, but we'd be leaving her alone in this forsaken place to swim it by herself. So she and I lower ourselves into the water and follow Miles. I want to cry for the sensation of water on my skin. It is . . . I can't even describe it.

It brings my mind back to the metal tub my mother poured kettle water into until it was warm enough for each of us children to bathe in. I can see the towels drying on the Sheila Maid hanging from the ceiling, dripping onto our floors as we giggled and danced around nude, awaiting our turn.

I go under the surface and see the tunnel, almost like a cave but filled with water. Miles and Kate are already swimming ahead, so I can't do anything but follow. As we slip through the burrow, I see runes on the walls, glowing.

I can read them now, with Sangreçu blood in my veins. They're warnings, but placed crookedly as if by a gloating hand that actually took pleasure in the thought of the danger it supposedly warned against.

We emerge into the grotto of the room with the sacrificial altar. I pull myself out of the water and run to it, water coursing off my dress. There doesn't seem to be any blood on the altar, thank God. I crouch down to see the capstone again covers the well. I fall to my knees and scramble to move it.

"No!" I cry.

It's set in place by magic. It's as if the spell repaired a rent in its gossamer with a few stitches and all is back as it was.

I hit my fist against it. My God, if time is running out . . . and where, where is the key? I had left it in the rock.

Horror dawns on me. The house doesn't want us to succeed. Did it kidnap Tabby as a distraction, so Phoebe wouldn't be able to come release Myrddin?

"Okay, she's not here," says Miles, and then, "Eleanor, are you all right?"

"No," I say. "Myrddin's under here. I had removed this capstone, and now it's back in place just as tight as before. And the key that opened the stone is missing."

"He's under *here?*" he asks.

"Yes! And if you and Phoebe hadn't disappeared to have relations with each other, the capstone might still be off!"

"I'm sorry," he says.

"You made love while my one chance at being released vanished!"

"We can come back and I'll help you with it," he promises.

"You don't understand," I say. "It's not just a heavy rock; it's fastened with *magic.*"

He stares at me, and my anger penetrates finally to him. "We're going to be stuck," I say. "We're not going to graduate. Even though we're all born on the same day and we're all Sangreçu, we're not going to achieve the prophecy. Because of *you two.*"

"Eleanor, we've got to find Tabby. That's our first job," says Kate. "She's still alive. We have to save her."

I stare down at the capstone, sick at heart. Yes, she's still alive, and Myrddin and Arthur and Nimue . . . they don't matter. They had their chance. They tangled their fates with terrible decisions and badly placed trust. The idea that Arthur can rise up and save England . . . from what I've seen, it doesn't need saving. No one wields swords anymore. The wars are over, or at least happening on some other soil. Phoebe and Miles have never talked of war. I don't think Miles has ever fought.

Everyone I've seen in England and France is just going about the task of living. The homes are not surrounded by barricades or moats against enemies. It's a different world than the one in which Myrddin vanished from view. It really doesn't matter that Arthur fell at Camlann, or that the yard contains a circle of swords abandoned by men who failed at their quest.

Right now, the only thing that matters is that little girl.

I steel myself to let Myrddin go. No one will ever locate that key again, and as long as the manor is in place, he will stand silent sentry in his empty well. He'll be nothing but a myth. The only ones who know where he lies: half of us are already dead.

Myrddin will recede to being the dragon in the margins of the old books. The marking on certain tombstones. And maybe someday Austin's cottage will be torn down to make a finer, newer home, and the bulldozer will not ask about the emblem.

Boswick will die, and his business cards with the golden foil on the dragon's forehead will be destroyed.

The spells that rest on my tongue will stay trapped there in my mouth. I'll forget them as soon as the Sangreçu wears off.

"Yes," I say dully. "Only Tabby matters."

I stand up and set my shoulders back. A servant is always good at adjusting to the whims of her masters and mistresses. Her own wants are of no importance. "It's faster if you and I intention," I say to Miles. "Kate can follow behind on foot."

"And where do we intention to?" he asks.

"The source of all this evil," I say. "The yew tree."

CHAPTER NINETEEN

Sometimes small cairns found near crossroads indicate
magical paths. The positioning of moss-covered stones
within the cairn provides another secretive sign for persons
knowledgeable in moss lore.

—*Secret Signs*, left out for Phoebe by Steven Arnaud

We get to the pond in time to see Tabby and Steven arrive. I sag in despair. He really did take Tabby—and his intent for her can't be any good.

Tabby's excited to see the pond. "Watta!" she cries delightedly. She's still dripping from her swim through the grotto, and I look at Steven in further anger that he made a child swim that tunnel.

I'm about to come forward, but I hear brush moving. A second later, Raven Gellerman emerges from the trail. "Finally," she says. "You managed to bring Tabby."

A chill walks up my spine.

She tries to pick Tabby up, but she hides behind her father's legs.

"Yes," says Steven.

"It took you long enough, didn't it?"

Miles and I look at each other and step out so we can be seen.

"Who the hell are you?" asks Steven.

"I'm Miles Whittleby. The one whose parents you were supposed to talk to. And this is Eleanor."

"You drank again," says Steven, and I hear the snarl in his voice. "I thought you and Phoebe found only one vial."

"Nice to meet you, too," says Miles.

"Take me to the vials. I'm an Arnaud and that's my property."

"Sure. Give me Tabby and we'll take you to them."

Tabby peers out from behind her father's legs and looks at Miles. She points at him. "He pick up."

She remembers him from Versailles. Miles throws me a grateful look and goes to Tabby with his arms open.

"I don't think so," says Steven. Tabby bats at his restraining arm. Miles kneels and smiles at Tabby, his arms at his sides. "Back off!"

"Phee friend," she says.

"Yes! I'm Phoebe's friend. Do you want me to take you to her?"

"Where are the vials?" Steven asks.

This is too much for me. "You care more about the vials than the chance to see your daughter!" I shout at him.

He looks confused. I walk over to him and reach out to touch his cheek.

Ah yes.

Ancient knowledge floods my body.

He's been marred.

He's half himself, and a darkness has embedded within him. He loves Phoebe fiercely—when he's himself.

"Take your hands off him!" snaps Raven.

I shove her away and take pleasure in seeing her stumble onto the ground. No one ever thinks the mild-mannered serving girl will pull a knife from her apron and use it. I have all kinds of violent acts I'm willing to engage in if the stakes are high enough.

"Stay down there," I order her. "Tabby, come with me and Miles."

Tabby stares up at me and her eyes are wide. But then they open wider, so wide it seems impossible. Her gaze shifts down. She's staring at something behind me that is blowing her mind.

I hear it behind me.

The surface of the water breaking. Something's emerging from the pond.

"Oh shite," says Miles in a low voice.

I turn around slowly. A few of the longest roots from the yew are now above the water, moving around like they are feeling for something.

More roots emerge, a dark, wet sinuous twining, as if a squid rests upside down on the bottom of the pond, its tentacles coming to the surface to seek prey.

"The scratches on their faces," says Miles to me.

This is what killed Alexander and Dee and Amey. Steven brought them here.

The roots sense us, all of them now stretching in our direction.

I turn, kick Steven in the groin with all my might, and snatch up Tabby as he bends over in pain. I don't turn back, because I know this kind of magic is potent and fast. It's a thousand times more powerful than me. I begin running but get only a few steps, slowed down by the child in my arms, before I feel the pulling at my skirts.

"Say a spell!" shouts Miles from my side.

The roots twine through my skirts and scratch my legs. In some distant and detached portion of my mind, I wonder if I can bleed now that I'm Sangreçu.

Miles is suddenly in front of me, and I pass Tabby to him.

He begins sprinting, but already I see the root extend past me, fat and ponderous.

I sort out the words spurting into my mind. I haven't said spells in so long that I can't control the onslaught of language, so I say all the words, even as the roots tug me backward. They pull me past Steven, and he looks relieved.

"Yes, take her!" he says.

I snag his pant leg as I go. "You're coming, too," I mutter, and my mouth again fills with panicked sputtering. I close my eyes to better help my mouth.

No one has said these words since the early beginnings of time. The air is surprised. The stones listen.

And the roots pause.

I complete the garble still sitting on my tongue. I hear rustling and sliding, the crackling as of kindling being gathered. The sound of thick, wooden fibers. I almost imagine them twisting and unfolding, like a snake wending in the grass. The sounds withdraw and get farther away. I still can't bear to turn around, but I feel the roots subsiding.

The silken sound of the grasses at the edge of the pond being disturbed.

The roots return to the water with a quiet plash.

I take in a breath with astounded elation. I pulled something out of the very blood in my veins, words that floated there, and saved us. I did . . . me. The servant who failed at her previous task.

Miles and Tabby are so far away I can't see them. And if Kate Darrow ever gets here, she'll have missed everything. Crawling over to straddle Steven, I press my hand to his forehead.

Again scrambling for words I once knew well, I utter the

spell of removal. This is an old and desperate spell that requires another receptacle for the darkness. So . . . where to put it?

I look at Raven pityingly, still following my command to stay on the ground, her fist in her mouth. It's not her fault. She's a pawn of larger forces, just as Steven is.

"Don't," she says, crawling backward.

My hand is raised in the air, pulsing with its horrid burden. In the past, I've released the darkness into someone already unhinged, like the man who won't wash and wanders the lanes spitting at an invisible foe. But I don't have such a person at hand.

I look around.

A black bird sits on a branch of a rowan tree, chattering and scolding, forthright in its indignation. Would it even work, I wonder? The old books never offered the chance to spill the darkness into a creature. But I want to try. If not Raven, then a raven.

My hand covers my view of the bird as I release the foulness at it.

It flies up into the sky, cursing and flying in deranged, aborted arcs. It comes to sit at my feet and its claws dig runes into the soil.

The runes spell out *hatred, murder, envy.*

I stretch out one hobnailed boot and erase the runes as soon as it makes them.

It caws at me, flies around my head, returns to the soil like a student to practice its letters again.

Hatred.

I erase it.

Hatred.

I erase it again, and for good measure kick at the bird, knowing it will fly off before my boot makes contact.

It flies off to the original rowan branch and stares down balefully. I see its talons restlessly dancing on the branch. It's still scratching out the runes.

Steven rises. He puts his arms around me and cries into my shoulder. His grief is stark and honest. I hold him up, feeling like my repair of him has actually brought him more pain.

Raven, her face showing all the shame it should, looks at me at length before getting up and running away as fast as she can.

"My own daughter," says Steven. "I tried to . . ." He breaks down and can't speak. His body shudders against mine. This is the worst kind of grief, with the weighty element of guilt.

"It wasn't you," I say.

"Who was it?"

I pause. "I'm not sure. I don't know."

"I gave it the others, but it only wanted her."

Coldness fills my veins. No matter the fact he wasn't himself, he has killed three people. And I inhale sharply as the second thought dawns. *The yew wanted Tabby specifically.*

"Cry later," I say roughly. "You need to tell your wife that you didn't succeed at killing your child."

CHAPTER TWENTY

Lying prostrate on the ground before the altar is a posture that demonstrates one's pure submission before God. With face to floor, we can be no more humble.

—www.handmaidnovice.com

*M*iles comes back for me. I've been watching the raven and scanning the surface of the pond. I'm not sure what I'm concerned about, exactly, but it seems important to keep vigil. The bird keeps scratching runes, and has added the tip of one wing as a writing instrument, which means he limps as he circles, off balance.

We put our hands on each other's shoulders and survey each other, like men do.

"All is well?" I ask.

"Tabby's clutching her mum and Phoebe so hard I think all their skin has fused together. Met Kate on the way in and she went back with us. I think she was scared to go into the woods herself, to be honest."

"With good reason. Did Steven make it back yet?"

"Not by the time I left. What happened here?"

"Spells. Temporary fighting off of evil. Steven's been cleansed until it gets to him again."

"Raven?"

"I don't think we'll see her again."

"You?"

"Still kicking. And yourself?"

"Finding myself strangely terrorized by trees."

I laugh. "That's our next job to tackle, since Steven let it slip that its overall intended victim is Tabby."

He lets go of me and steps back, his eyes alarmed. "Why?"

"Honestly, I haven't a clue. I've thought it over again and again. Athénaïs told us Tabby wasn't important. She wasn't firstborn, and she isn't an October 20 baby."

"But."

"Exactly. But."

"I think Athénaïs is Nimue," he says. "At Versailles, she told Phoebe they shared the same soul. If Phoebe is Nimue, then she was Athénaïs, too."

I nod, thinking. "She knew all kinds of sorcery. Perhaps under the tutelage of Myrddin."

"Changing her name through the centuries. She told me she had had many names," says Miles. "And she said she would follow Madame Arnaud to England, and we were told she disappeared."

"So she changed her name? Lived here?"

He shrugs.

I reach out and tug one of those black tufts of his hair. The opposite of Austin's golden hair.

"What if . . ." I say, thinking aloud. "The same way that Nimue stole Myrddin's secrets and trapped him, Madame Arnaud stole her secrets and trapped her?"

"Her, as in Athénaïs?"

"Yes."

"Was there another person in that well?"

"Ah, Miles," I say with a grudging laugh. "Glad you're taking all this so seriously."

"But I'm sure that reminds you of something."

"If we can drag her away from her family," I say.

"I think she owes you," he says.

Phoebe and I crouch before the capstone. I don't have the key, but. if she can remember the spell, she can undo it.

The sound of relentlessly dripping water surrounds us.

"I'm sorry, Eleanor," she says quietly.

I don't answer. I am listening to the sound below me, the slow heart encased in armor. It barely beats. It is as unhurried as the cadence of myths.

I lie down on my stomach, to get our two hearts closer. He can borrow mine. It doesn't move anymore but he can have it. My cheek to the stone floor, I listen. It is the saddest stillness. It makes me wish I wasn't Sangreçu so I couldn't hear it.

She lies down, too. We must look like two nuns prostrated before the altar.

"I'm sorry, too," I say.

I ask Kate to make me tea. I crave its solace, and it gives her a job to do. She and I are both disappointed that Anne's tea consists of dried gray flakes in a tissue bag on a string. I sniff it and it is barely aromatic. When the steaming cup is set before me, however, next to the last book Steven set out with a false lead to follow, I nearly swoon. I take a sip and scorch my tongue, and take another sip to bathe the burn.

Pain. Flavor.

Exquisite.

"What happened down there?" Kate asks.

"She didn't remember the spell," I say. I glance at Anne, clutching Tabby on her lap, shell-shocked at the sight of me, the dead servant girl sitting at her table. "But that's all right; Miles is comforting her."

Kate bites her lip at my bitter tone.

"Miles is?" Anne repeats. She rubs her forehead. Hard enough, I suppose, for a mother to accept her daughter seeking romance with a lad she barely knows, but adding in the fact that he's dead and her child's dead must make her feel a dull panic. "But *you* need comforting."

I take another brutally hot swallow. "As do you," I tell her. "We need to talk about your husband. Phoebe told me he locked himself in the car."

Anne's eyes fill with tears. "I think he felt it was the safest place, that he wouldn't harm us if he was in a separate space away from the manor and its estate."

I nod, although privately I think metal and glass won't protect him if the house's evil wants him. "I went and gave him a sickness spell—nothing too strong—to keep him from going anywhere while we take care of . . . what's in the pond. I think you know what's in the pond?"

Her hand snakes out to cover her mouth as she begins to sob.

"Mommy?" asks Tabby.

Kate and I silently drink our tea while Anne struggles to control her emotions. I had considered giving her a draught of forgetfulness, but to keep her on her guard I felt she needed to know the deeds Steven was capable of..

"Would you like me to put Tabby to bed for you, so that you and Eleanor can talk?" Kate offers.

"No!" says Anne.

I look pityingly at Tabby, her eyes red with exhaustion. She *should* go to sleep, but I don't think her mother will release a grasp on her until they are far, far from this horrible manor.

"He's a good man," I say. "No one can resist the darkness once it worms its way inside."

"And you completely destroyed the darkness in him?"

I hesitate. "Yes. But it could take up residence again. So we still have to determine what is sending it."

"He brought us here," she says shakily. "He was already under the influence then."

"I don't know."

"It wants . . ." Her eyes shift downward with a subtle nod to indicate her daughter.

"It seems that way."

"We have to go. We'll go back to the U.S."

Suddenly Phoebe is with us. She stands behind her mother, bending to wrap her arms around her and Tabby both.

"Phee!" cries Tabby.

"Close your eyes and try to sleep," says Anne to her youngest, but Tabby knows better than the rest of us that if she stops looking at her sister, she may never see her again.

Miles arrives and smiles awkwardly. If he thinks staggering their entrances fools any of us, he is wrong.

"We have something to do before the Sangreçu effects subside," I say.

"Can't it wait until morning?" Phoebe asks. "Maybe in the night I'll remember the spell for you."

I bite my tongue until blood fills my mouth. So careless of Nimue, to destroy a life and then forget the words that accomplished it. I pick up the cup of tea and drink it down.

"We'll commence a study of spells as soon as we fix things for the living," I say. "Come on."

CHAPTER TWENTY-ONE

Much like a tarot deck, the runes do not give an explicit and unambiguous message. Instead, the diviner must listen to the symbols and reach through the wood, stone, or what the delivery material is, to hear the intention of the cipher.

—*Divination Practices*

*I*t's dark now, and candles and lanterns light our work as Phoebe drains the pond. She's the water woman, the Lady of the Lake. She frowns to remember, but then it's an easy chain of words and gestures for her.

The water recedes.

Against the sky, the silhouette looms. We see the full power of the yew on its side. It's grown since the last time I saw it, monstrously large. As large as the limits of the pond.

And entangled in its branches and roots are the bodies, scratched to the utmost by a greedy force.

The runes don't glow but instead appear to be burned into the wood. I approach, my shoes sinking in the murk. I can read their message now: *She is here.* Is the *she* Tabby?

At the limits of the lost lake stand the rest of the party, loath to come closer. With the exception of Steven, restlessly sleeping in the car with the fever I foisted on him, all the Arnauds are here, as well as Miles. Tabby is thankfully asleep at this hour in her mother's arms. Even Kate Darrow stands ready to assist; she's seen too much to not be included.

"Do we set fire to it?" I ask. No one answers.

"We should give these people a decent burial," says Anne.

"Not one of them," says Phoebe, pointing to Madame Arnaud, whose black skirts have become like lace by the stretching and tormenting of the tree. I walk closer and see that her eyes have rolled into the back of her head, leaving egg whites peering out at me vengefully. Unsettled, I retreat to stand with the others near the flames, throughout the centuries our weapon against the night.

"But the rest of them," Anne insists.

"How do we do that?" Miles asks.

"That man . . . the one who tried to buy us off," says Anne slowly. "He tried to stop the bulldozer."

She shifts the sleeping child in her arms as her words come in an inspired burst. "He wants to keep all of this quiet. That's his aim. So he'll enlist the help of all the people who put together money to keep us from renovating the property, and some of the police must be in on it, or he'll pay them off, and they'll get the bodies back to their families. He'll figure it out: what to say, how to do it."

I marvel at her calm reasoning in the face of everything she's endured: not just today, but in the months since her elder daughter's death. She has the backbone of a queen.

"I don't think we should burn it," says Phoebe suddenly.

"Why not?" I ask.

"Because the villagers would've burned it if they thought it would work."

"Good point," says Miles. "But cutting it down and drowning didn't seem to be all that effective, either."

"It was effective," she says. "As long as Madame Arnaud was around."

"Or," I say slowly. "Effective until Tabby arrived."

Everyone turns to look at her, slumped in the sleep of the innocent.

"We'll go," says Anne. "Tonight. I don't give a damn about any of our things. Needless to say, I don't want to renovate the Arnaud Manor anymore."

"Mom . . . are you taking Steven with you?" asks Phoebe.

"I can't," says Anne. "I believe Eleanor when she says he was the victim of dark magic, but I can't forget that he tried to—" Her voice falters.

"Steven can't stay here, though," says Miles. "It will work its way into him again."

"You'll have to lie," says Kate. "Take him back to the States with you, and then detach from him."

"I don't think I can," says Anne. "It would be too hard."

Phoebe starts to cry.

"You have to get him as far away as possible from this estate," I say to her firmly. "It will be hard, but it's for Tabby's sake."

Anne leans her head down onto Phoebe's head and closes her eyes. "They say many marriages end in divorce after a child dies," she says quietly. "I had hoped to beat that statistic."

It sinks in. Boswick will get his way after all. He can rebuild the wall that blocks the driveway. He'll let the archeologists catalog the swords, maybe take them away, maybe rebury them.

I stare bleakly at the yew and its horrifying litter of corpses.

What will Boswick tell their families? What explanation will satisfy them?

Ages have passed since Myrddin learned his protégée, his beautiful partner, had lain with the king, also his protégé.

How world-weary he must have felt, that the young lives he shaped so lovingly turned away from him and toward each other. This one detail—their love—changed *everything*, caused him to become enchanted and thus Camelot to fall, Arthur impotent without his counsel and magic. And yet this detail never made it into the chronicles.

Today, the fragments and remnants of those long-ago people find a way to lodge in the new generation, through bloodlines and genetics and pure, inexplicable magic. Calendar pages flickering in the fire. Whoever chooses the identity of the babe growing in its mother's womb?

Would Myrddin have been angered to be recast as a female servant despite the monumental maleness of him? Miles and Phoebe kept their genders . . . why did I change?

I smile ruefully at the simple answer. Because Myrddin was always a shape-shifter and trickster.

Some of us carried through, but not others. Launcelot, Galahad, Bors, and Perceval: their lives perhaps continue in some vaunted sunburst hall where the Grail radiates and holds them in a beautiful thrall of purity. Guinevere, although her loveliness was distracting, had no life after her death. I continued, and continue, as does Arthur on his island and Nimue wherever she lies, whatever Madame Arnaud did to her.

So Tabby must be another who carried through. I just don't know her genesis and her meaning.

I probably never will. There's nothing I can do. I will linger in this state forever. Forever wondering.

As I look at Tabby, she rouses in her mother's arms. She lifts her head up and looks directly at me.

Directly.

Her arm comes off Anne's neck. She's got something clenched in her little palm. She reaches out to me.

"What is it?" I murmur.

I step closer and she smiles sleepily at me, her face half lit by the flickering light of the lanterns.

She opens her fist and shows me. The golden capstone key.

"Key," she says.

ACKNOWLEDGMENTS

Thanks in a heartfelt way go to Mary Volmer; Alison Mc-
Mahan; Gina L. Mulligan; Jennifer Laam; Erin McCabe;
Ian Wilson; Clara, Reid, and Alan; Michaela Hamilton,
Lauren Jernigan, Karen Auerbach, Randie Lipkin, and Ar-
thur Maisel.

Many thanks to the Chaucer Middle English Glossary
online, which I relied on to create the prophecy. It is fun
to click around at www.literature-dictionary.org/Chaucers-
Middle-English-Glossary. Also huge thanks to beautiful
writer Essie Fox for helping my English characters sound as
English as possible.

If you loved this book, it'd be really helpful (and appreciated!) if you posted a review online or told a friend about
it. It will boost your chances to become Sangreçu someday.

**Just in case you missed the first book
in the Arnaud Legacy trilogy,
here is a sample excerpt . . .**

Told from the point of view of
PHOEBE IRVING

*Y*ou know you've done something pretty awful when your family moves because of it. Not just within San Francisco, nor within California . . . not even within the country.

My stepdad, Steven, has a remote job, so it was no problem for him to relocate. Mom is a stay-at-home mom for Tabby; her job "traveled," too. As for me, they unenrolled me from school just a month before sophomore year ended.

Crazy.

When you're a major screwup, it helps if your stepdad has an ancestral mansion in England ready to move into. Well, not exactly *ready*. It's been uninhabited for a long time and needs some serious TLC, I heard him tell Mom.

He'd been trying to sell it for years. But at least it's a place to live, and a place for me to reflect on my behavior and improve it.

My therapy would be a lot more effective if I could remember what I did.

Emerging from the tunnel of trees to the clearing where we could finally see my stepfather's manor, I let out a moan of disillusionment. This wasn't the crumbling but still-impressive castle surrounded by broad, grassy lawns I'd imagined back in California, with swans wafting snootily around a lily-ponded lake. Instead, it was a grim, stone-walled prison with the grounds so overgrown they were nearly impenetrable.

I had allowed myself to become interested, had thought there was a lovely poetry to the phrase, "ancestral mansion in England." But nothing could quell the immediate sense of grinding apprehension the manor gave me. Nothing about it felt right.

As we drove up into its shadow, the manor leaned down over us to look. More than idly curious, it practically rubbed its leathern hands together in glee. *Visitors. At last.*

It was built in the shape of a U, making it hard to see where exactly one of the wings ended since it was lost somewhere to our left in a thick group of trees. The central courtyard that we inched along was cobblestoned, the size of a grand but cheerless park.

"Um, how many ancestors did you *have?*" I asked.

"It does seem large for one family," Steven answered, sighing and looking at Mom. "The Arnauds were very powerful and wealthy in the early 1700s when this was built."

"And the size of our family . . ." said Mom. Steven reached over and touched her cheek.

"We'll make it work," he said. He parked the car, turned off the engine, and got out. Mom sat there for a while, then turned around to check on Tabitha, my little sister, still sleeping in her car seat.

I got out and looked up at the Arnaud house while Steven started pulling luggage out of a hard plastic carrier atop the car. When I looked all the way to the top of the manor, my neck strained with the effort, my head hanging back heavily. *God, how big is this place?* There were hundreds of windows, dozens of gables, and a million stone designs of birds and beasts carved into the dark stone walls.

The manor's heavy breath stirred the hairs on the back of my neck. It surveyed me. It examined Mom and Steven and Tabby. Each of the windows looked smeared with time, but it seemed like the house could still see through them.

It would be easy to get lost in a house that size—and no one would find you.

I turned around and looked at the surrounding forest, ragged with illicit shrubs. It didn't look like any gardeners came to take care of this overwrought mess.

"No neighbors?" Mom asked.

Steven shook his head. "I think the original landhold-
ings were even larger. There's no one else around for
miles. This is the only house on Auldkirk Lane."

Mom unbuckled Tabby and pulled her out. "Welcome
to your new home, sweetie," she said. My little sister
rubbed her gray eyes, which were huge in her tiny face.
She was wearing a headband with a pink flower on it,
crooked from her nap. When she turned her head to
look at the manor, I could see a tuft of snarled auburn
hair in the back.

Steven grabbed the biggest suitcase, my mom's. I expected him to head toward the double wooden doors
that clearly marked the main entry, but he ducked into a
smaller door on the right wing, marked with a small
stone roof.

"You'll be relieved," he called over his shoulder, "to
see our quarters aren't quite as ancient as the rest of the
house. The information the real estate people sent me
was that there is a very comfortable living space in the
east wing."

Mom and Tabby went inside directly behind him, and
I heard Mom coo in amazement. I hesitated outside, un-
willing to go through the portal and enter the house's influence. I waited, listening to the wind sing through the
tree canopy. This was our new home. Because of me.

I lowered my head and followed them in—and saw
why Mom was so surprised.

It was completely modern inside. Well, modern as of
the 1970s. The living room had plaid and leather sofas,
adorned with small circular pillows. The rug was a shag

sunrise, as the colors moved in a rippling line from pale yellow to bright gold. Giant orbs hung on linked chains from the ceiling, hovering over the furniture to provide lighting.

Mom and I walked into the kitchen, which had avocado-colored appliances. With a little smile, she tried out the stove's gas burners. "Well, at least I won't have to use a cauldron," she murmured.

Behind the kitchen was a den, with a pigeonholed desk, a leather armchair, and a standing floor lamp whose lampshade was decorated with orange and brown stripes.

I looked for the bedrooms next. Oddly, there was a nursery with a crib and a dresser with waddling ducks painted on each drawer. I had to think: Had Steven said he'd been born in this house? Maybe this had been his room once.

The master bedroom, oversized and smelling slightly stuffy, was clearly not for me.

My room had a twin bed covered in a bright green spread, with matching carpet. If the room had windows, I was sure the drapes would have been the same glaring green. The effect was that I was a worm who'd burrowed into the dark heart of a lime.

On the plus side, the room was as large as a master suite, and the tiny bed viewed from the door looked like a forgotten slipper in a queen's dressing room. My room in California had been pretty small; this had possibility. I could have a lot of friends over. That is, if I could make some here in Grenshire.

I didn't mind leaving behind my stuff; everything was

from IKEA anyway. Maybe Mom and I could cruise yard sales and do a shabby chic thing for my room.

A mirror hung above the dresser. I didn't look that bad, considering everything I'd been through. My long auburn hair was still reasonably wavy and I didn't need concealer to hide circles under my green eyes.

I'm not a knockout but last year I did manage to snag one of the hottest guys in school, Richard Spees. Total surprise here, because guys don't stop in the school hallway and pivot to keep their eyes on girls like me. I've seen that happen a lot, but always to someone else.

Luckily, I'm an athlete—a swimmer—so at least I don't worry about my weight, although I would really, really like to get rid of that one huge mole right in my cleavage. What little there is of that, that is. I definitely fail the pencil test Bethany told me about—it's when you put a pencil horizontally under your boob and see if it stays by itself.

I read constantly, and subsequently have the kind of vocabulary that makes English teachers' eyes light up (which doesn't exactly help with the guys, but I can't prevent the stuff that comes out of my mouth). Last year I took a creative writing class, and found something I thought I could be good at. I could be a swimming author. A literary mermaid.

I sat down on the edge of the bed. I didn't mind the color scheme, but the room had hardly any light. Why no windows? It sucked not to be able to get some fresh air. Maybe whoever designed this was worried about teens sneaking out the window at night.

I returned to the living room with a big sigh. "My room's acid green," I announced. No one said anything, and I gritted my teeth. They would see it as a complaint, and here I was trying to be a better daughter. Mom and Steven's parenting technique: ignores anything verging on whining. "It's okay," I amended. "Green's good."

Still no response.

"I'm sorry," I said.

Steven rescued me. "Any interest in seeing the rest of the house?" he asked, holding up what looked like floor plans.

"Yeah," I said. I gave him a big smile, but he wasn't ready to return it. Parents are so big on that punishment thing.

"Not right now," said Mom. "You go along. I'll stay with Tabby."

"You sure?" he asked.

"Yes," she said. "My guess is, it's not the safest place for babies. You scout it out first."

"I don't imagine it's babyproofed," he said drily, and she laughed.

"Tell me if you see those medieval outlet covers," she said.

"Medieval? It's not that old," he protested.

"Could've fooled me," she said with a grin.

"All right," he said. "If I'm not back in an hour, call the fire department because I've probably fallen through a rotten floorboard."

"That's all I need," she said. "Seriously, be safe."

He kissed her and Tabby, and went back outside, with

me following behind. The air was a little cooler now that it was late afternoon. I straightened my back; was someone watching me? It didn't help that the light was fading prematurely thanks to the intense foliage. The shadows of leaves agitated by the wind made strange patterns on the ground.

"Twilight at the haunted mansion," Steven intoned in a deep voice, and then he chuckled.

"Not so funny," I said. "There's a legitimate creep factor here."

He led me toward those big main doors I had seen before, and pulled from his pocket an enormous, antique-looking key. A man's anguished face made of iron was the lock; the key went into his open mouth. He looked like he was in the midst of a scream, and the key was meant to be his gag.

The doors were heavy. Steven's face turned red as he pushed one of them inward. It groaned like it hadn't been opened in centuries.

"Are you sure we should go in?" I asked.

"It'll be good to get some fresh air circulating," he said quietly.

Inside, *holy crap*. Huge. Dynastically huge. The entry hall with its vaulted ceiling was so large I could have thrown a rock with all my strength and it would only get halfway across the floor. The stones forming the floor were arranged in patterns of dark gray and lighter gray, creating a somber chessboard stretching into the distance.

The grand staircase at the other end was wide enough to hold dozens of people on each riser, and the chandelier hovering over us was so full of glass and iron that if it fell it would plow through the bedrock beneath the flooring, like a meteor. Most of one wall was taken up by a fireplace large enough to roast several standing horses—you know, if you ever wanted to.

The air felt museumlike. Cold. I tried to imagine the hall filled with life, lots of people in high ruffled collars smiling and laughing, and the sound of carriages rolling up to the entry outside, but all I could think was that all of them were long dead, and their dresses and breeches had rotted into sticky threads.

"Hello!" shouted Steven to the ceiling. It echoed back at him seconds later.

I wished he hadn't done that. It seemed—I don't know—just wrong somehow. He started toward the stairs, and when he was halfway there, I ran to catch up with him. The run was long enough that I was out of breath when I got there—and I'm the girl who can hold her breath. My lungs are hard as canteens from all my years of swimming.

I practically needed my passport to cross that room. The leaded glass windows, at varying levels in the walls, let in a filtered sunlight that made the place more disturbing. Gigantic cobwebs, or maybe they were spiderwebs, hung everywhere, stretched between light sconces like an ethereal tapestry.

The stairs were steep but seemed to draw me upward. *Come in, come in.*

I remembered my initial aversion to entering the manor . . . and now I was climbing up into its timeworn center. Some sort of invitation was being issued to me. Something lonely was made glad by our visit.

Steven climbed ahead of me; I kept some distance between us in case he started to fall. I didn't want to be a pair of dominoes with him.

Halfway up, I turned and looked down. Vertigo overcame me as I wavered there on the steps. For a second I was so sure I was going to fall that I clutched for the banister, furred with grime. After I steadied myself, I rubbed my hands on my jeans.

At the top of the stairs, I took a good look at the stained glass window that presided over the landing. Etched at the bottom was xxx, which made me snort because the image depicted was hardly X-rated. It showed two medieval knights. One was thrusting a spear into the other, who was rearing up with his sword. It looked like the one being impaled was going to seriously damage the other one when the sword came down.

Steven turned left, where he opened another set of double doors. We entered what had once been a ballroom. The curtains covering the floor-to-ceiling windows hung in shreds, their fibers simply too old to keep their shape against the sun's endless onslaught. The floor was a black-and-white marble parquet.

A trickle of sweat rolled from my temple. I felt like we were trespassing and were about to get caught at any minute. I wished Steven would walk a little more softly, but his heavy oxford shoes created their own small echo.

At the other end of the long room was an organ, large

as a church's. It dominated the space, looking like a miniature factory with all its pipes and bellows.

Steven took off his sweatshirt and used it to sweep dust off the organ bench. A cloud enveloped him and he began sneezing. "This better be worth it," he said. "I actually really like this shirt." His voice sounded brittle in the huge space.

He sat down and began pushing his feet alternately on two large, slanted wooden panels on the floor. I could hear a sort of wheeze or breath deep within the organ as it came to life. He pressed down one of the keys. Nothing happened, but as he continued to work the pedals, he pressed again and a slender noise came. As he pumped life into the mechanism, music emerged, his fingers moving swiftly over the keys, jumping from octave to octave. He performed something I recognized from the classical music station he always played in the car.

He pulled a round lever that said VOX HUMANA and the sound instantly changed, became eerily like monks singing in the distance, their voices drifting up from the monastery walls.

"I didn't know you could play," I said. He was a master, and I'd never seen him so much as look at a piano before, other than Tabby's four-key toy in the shape of a blue hippopotamus.

"God, it's been a long time," he said. He pressed another pedal and the sound became louder.

"You'll wake the dead," I said. I leaned over his right shoulder and tried to play my own chord. To his credit, he didn't try to rearrange my fingers like my old piano teacher used to. But he had already stopped working the pedals, so I didn't get to hear how monstrous and discordant my guess was.

The profound silence of the vast house settled around us. I had the strange feeling that the house or maybe the organ had not appreciated his sudden, forceful playing . . . as if he hadn't been respectful.

Please, get real, I told myself. *The house isn't angry at us.*

Steven stood up and the organ bench gave a stilted screech at the redistribution of weight. He tied his filthy sweatshirt around his waist and led me through an arched wooden door set in the side wall.

This next room was probably as big as the ballroom, but divided into three levels of bookshelves, ascending all the way up to the ceiling. The number of books was overpowering, and so was their odor. They were moldering, page by page, moisture making its way from the prefaces all the way through to the epilogues. Railings fenced in the three levels, making them resemble Spanish balconies. Narrow, rickety staircases—almost more like ladders— led up to each floor.

I climbed one of the staircases to see what kind of books rich people read in the 1700s. At the top level, I looked down at Steven, noticing the bald spot that his height normally hid, at least from me. He was reading the titles on one of the shelves, so I did the same, turning randomly to stare at the spines. Surprise: they were in French. But as I walked carefully across the balcony I saw some English titles, too, like *The Governance of Servants* and *Quelling Insubordination.*

After I came down, we walked room to room in silence, as if a deaf-mute real estate agent led us. The glut of rooms was dizzying: some chambers elevated by a few steps, others sunken. The house was a beehive with these dark interlocking cells. I imagined a gigantic queen bee, mistress of the hive, loping ahead of us, dragging her useless wings, to not be seen.

Once, after consulting his map, Steven knelt at a paneled wall and exposed what looked to be a cupboard but was actually the beginning of a passageway. After staring into its black depths for a moment, he closed it and said, "No, thanks." I laughed in agreement. Too claustrophobic.

At times, he jogged forward; at times, I had to stop and wait for him. I kept imagining hearing the swish of those giant bee wings, or maybe more like the sound of skirts, the way a small train would drag along the floor.

Somehow we emerged back in the great hall. It took me a second to recognize it from the different perspective.

"And that was just one wing of the house," said Steven. "Holy Christ."

I raised my eyebrows. Steven didn't usually swear in front of me. "You want to do the rest?" I asked. "I'm not tired."

He matter-of-factly folded his floor plans up and tucked them under his arm. "We'll save the rest for a rainy day," he said.

★ ★ ★

We went back to the apartment, where Mom and Tabby were playing with spoons on the living room floor. They hadn't been able to bring many of her toys, so apparently the flatware drawer was the new Babies R Us.

Now that I knew some of what lay beyond the zany brightness of these 1970s walls, I found it wasn't as easy to relax as before. Decay breathed behind the macramé. *That's pretty good,* I thought. *"Decay breathed behind the macramé." I could use that in a story.*

"What's it like?" asked Mom. Steven sat down on the floor next to her while I crashed on the sofa. For Tabby's amusement, he began drawing lines in the shag's pile with a soup spoon.

"Huge. Beautiful in a really decrepit way."

"So it won't be easy to make a showplace out of it."

He snorted. "It would be the project of the century."

"Sounds like just what we need," she said.

He snorted again.

"No, honestly," she said. "I need something to focus on. Anything we could sell to fund a renovation?"

"There's quite the library," said Steven. "I should get a rare books expert in here to inventory it."

"How come your mom didn't?" she asked.

"A commonsense thing like that would never have occurred to her. And she was never here long enough to put something like that into action." I saw the muscle at his jaw clench, just for a second.

He didn't like to talk about his mom. I had never met her.

"How long did she live here?" I asked.

"She and my father lived here less than a year, I think. She got pregnant with me, and he was abusive, so she fled back to the States to protect both of us."

My jaw dropped. I had never heard this. And from the look on Mom's face, neither had she. Steven was secretive about his family.

"He died soon afterward, so he was a nonevent as far as I'm concerned," Steven added.

"I'm really sorry," I said lamely. I didn't know what else to say. I was lucky that although my parents had separated, it wasn't until I was ten. And pretty much immediately Steven was on the scene, so I never went dadless.

"For anyone who would lift a hand to a child," said Steven, "death is a good answer."

"You mean . . . he hit her when she was pregnant?" Mom asked.

"That's what she told me."

That was a weird way to answer, especially with the tone of voice he used. He stared down at the runes his spoon had made. "Well, anyway, ancient history. It makes me think about the life I might've had if he was a different person. That nursery was meant for me, you know; I would have been raised as an Arnaud heir on the palatial grounds of his forebears."

"Would you have wanted to?" she asked dubiously.

"Well, things were much more in order back then," he

said. "The estate has been neglected for as long as I've been alive."

Personally, I didn't think the manor's crumbling was just from the last half century . . . things had been declining here for *way* longer than that.

"It's sad not to know your father," said Steven. "And that's the last I'm going to say on that."

Mom nodded wistfully, glancing over at me on the sofa. This was as much info on his family as we'd ever gotten. Mom had once warned me not to ask. It didn't make sense to press for more. He'd talk when he wanted to.

That night, I went to my lime-colored room. On a whim, I opened the dresser drawers to see neatly folded piles of my clothing. I hadn't had time to unpack, but Mom, God bless her, had done it for mc. She must've filled the drawers while Steven and I were exploring the house. A little unnerved, I searched for my diary until I found it, still safely locked with the key in the toe of my candy-cane Christmas socks.

I sat down on my bed and let my mind drift back into a memory: Richard Spees stopping by our table in the cafeteria.

He's a senior and hot beyond belief. He stands right beside me, and I'm immediately thinking, *No way! He's standing by me?* Uma freezes, her french fry, coated with ketchup, halfway to her mouth. I straighten my posture and tuck my hair behind my ears.

"Hey, Phoebe, you looked good yesterday," he says.

"You were there?"

"I was."

"Thanks," I say, wishing I could come up with something cooler. Yesterday had been the swim meet against Oakland High. I'd torched them in the 100-meter freestyle, touching the wall what seemed like hours before anyone else. I think about how I must have looked from his eyes as I launched myself out of the pool in my school-colors-red-and-gold Speedo (last year, a few of us had petitioned for sexier, yet still aerodynamic, suits) and took all the high fives and wet hugs from my teammates. Finding out he had been looking at me when I didn't even know it makes me feel self-conscious.

"You looked good," he repeats, and suddenly I see it as a compliment to my body, rather than a sports-based comment on my performance.

I'm not going to say I completely take it in stride, because that doesn't happen. My cheeks burn with a really big blush, but I do manage to give a huge and hopefully sassy grin. Luckily, Bethany rescues me.

"Do you usually go to the swim meets?" she asks.

I throw her a grateful look, but before he can answer, she adds, "Or was there someone there you wanted to see?" I try to kick her under the table but get only her chair leg. She jolts backward a half inch in her plastic seat and laughs.

As I wait mortified for his response, it happens.

Stars swim up from behind my eyes, lazy and spectacular, taking the place of Bethany's gleeful face. The stars convey lightning bolts, too, and I'm dazzled and trying not to get hit. It's a slow lightning storm across the landscape of my vision, and as air creeps into my lungs, I submit.

Bethany tells me later that Richard said meaningfully, "There *was* someone I wanted to see," but all hell broke loose and people were yelling.

I wake up a few minutes after I passed out, Bethany says. Dozens of people cluster around me, and I'm lying facedown on the table. Ketchup from Uma's fries coats my hair. I raise my head, and the cafeteria aide helps me walk to the nurse's office.

I had fainted. Pretty dramatically.

It didn't cost me Richard Spees, even though I'd drooled while I was unconscious. "It didn't look great," admitted Bethany when I'd pressed her. Plus, there had been that ketchup masquerading as hair gel. Yet Richard had risen above all his gentlemanly disgust and somehow considered me attractive, even while lifting me from the table like a beached jellyfish and slapping me.

We dated for three excruciating months. He turned out to be a darb (dramatically asinine random boy) who prattled on and on until I had to admit my two-year-old sister was a more insightful conversationalist. But I was glad I dated him; I learned some skills I could put to better use with some other guy down the road. The kind of skills you have to write in code in your diary in case your mom reads it.

The memory was over.

I brushed my teeth in the bathroom (my own! Score one for England!) by the light of the 1970s big-eyed owl night-light. The wallpaper was gold foil depicting wheat stalks: so retro.

I pulled back the jade-colored bedspread and got in bed. I missed my quilt from home, a red and white thing my grandma made from a pattern in a book of Amish quilts.

I lay there looking at the ceiling, the kind of plaster that shows semicircular sweeps from some kind of tool. Like little white rainbows. I counted them. Wasn't sure if I should count the half sweeps over by the walls.

Come on, you must be tired, go ahead and sleep, I coached myself.

I was drifting restlessly when I heard the organ. It was playing low and quiet, a plodding, rhythmic bit of music, so subtle I thought for a while it was just noise in my head.

When I realized what I was hearing, I sat bolt upright, my heart pounding. The music seemed to disappear the more I concentrated on listening, like trying to figure out what a newscaster is saying on TV a room away.

I wandered out to the living room, where Steven was reading. The room was dark and he sat in the light cast by the gigantic hanging orb. Mom must have already gone to bed.

"Did you hear that?" I asked him.

His gaze didn't waver from the page. He was like that; he'd get caught up in whatever he was reading

"I thought I heard that organ playing, Steven," I said louder. "Do you think there's someone else in the house?"

He closed the book, letting it lie in his lap, and rubbed his face with both hands. Exhausted. Maybe sad. "Just forget about it," he said. "Let it go."

"Seriously? But if there's someone in the house . . ."

He sighed. He knew how to make gestures like that speak volumes. That sigh said, *You're a hysterical teenager, chill out.*

Insulted, I almost said something pissy, but I stopped myself. We had moved to England because of me. I had done something so very, very awful that we had to leave the country. If he didn't think the organ was anything to worry about, it wasn't anything to worry about.

"Okay," I said with a little smile. "They'll come for you first."

He grimaced.

I had imagined the organ because I was jet-lagged and out of sorts. Freaked out about living in a different house, a different continent. I went back down the hallway, opening the door to my own personal scarab-green room.

I lay down on the bed and closed my eyes, but I didn't sleep. I couldn't relax enough.